THE SECRET
OF THE
CRAZY QUILT

FLORENCE HIGHTOWER

THE
SECRET OF
THE
CRAZY QUILT

Illustrated by Beth and Joe Krush

Houghton Mifflin Company Boston 1972

Also by
FLORENCE HIGHTOWER

Dark Horse of Woodfield
Fayerweather Forecast
The Ghost of Follonsbee's Folly
Mrs. Wappingers's Secret

LIBRARY OF CONGRESS CATALOG CARD NUMBER 72-184247
ISBN 0-395-13729-2
PRINTED IN THE UNITED STATES OF AMERICA
FIRST PRINTING W

CONTENTS

THE SECRET
OF THE
CRAZY QUILT

Jerusha's Narrative

Arrival

I WAS THIRTEEN and Freddy was eight in June 1926 when we traveled alone from Chicago to Sewell, Massachusetts. We had made the trip lots of times before, but always with our parents. I was worried I would miss a connection right up until we had made the last change at Houghton Junction and got on the 5:32 P.M. local to Sewell. We stashed our overnight cases in the luggage rack — our trunk had been sent ahead — turned one seat back to front and, with a whole double seat each, spread ourselves out, feet up, facing each other.

"We made it," I said, "and I didn't even get a nosebleed."

I was subject to nosebleeds, always at embarrassing times and places.

"I thought you'd have one for sure when you couldn't find your pocketbook on the sleeper." Freddy giggled. "I was waiting for it to pour all over the porter when he fished the pocketbook out from under the bunk and gave it to you."

I snatched up the pocketbook from the seat beside me and clamped it between my knees so I wouldn't lose it again. I wasn't used to carrying a pocketbook. I'd always carried money, when I had any, in my bloomer leg.

Freddy jabbed his finger at the pocketbook. "The gum," he shouted. "Remember the gum! We're safe on the train and nothing to worry about. You promised."

I rummaged two sticks of O-Boy gum out of the pocketbook and gave one to Freddy. "Practice while you can," I said. "It's probably your last chance this summer."

"You mean because of Aunt Edith? Grandma wouldn't have minded."

I was about to tear the wrapper off my own stick of O-Boy, when that reminder that Grandma wasn't in Sewell, was, in fact, dead, hit me in the stomach. I didn't want any gum.

"Here." I handed mine to Freddy.

"Gee, Jerry, thanks. It's a lot easier to practice bubbles with two sticks than one. Gee, you're swell. Are you sure you're all right?" Freddy looked at my nose. I nodded and turned to the window so he wouldn't see the tears that were welling in my eyes.

I hadn't wanted to come to Sewell that summer without my parents, but Mama's lungs were kicking up again.

"If your mother doesn't have complete rest in a sanatorium in the mountains this summer," Daddy had said, "she may never get well. I can't pay her bills and send you and Freddy to camp too, and I can't let the two of you kick around Chicago all summer in the heat, exposed to scarlet fever and infantile paralysis and heaven knows what all. You know how your mother worries. Her rest in the mountains wouldn't do her any good at all. Edith has asked you both to Sewell. She needs you to help her cheer up Grandpa. He's been very low since Grandma died."

"She needs Freddy," I said. "Not me."

Daddy rubbed his forehead. I had an inspiration.

"I won't kick around," I said. "I'll stay indoors and keep house for you. I'll cook and clean and sew and bring you your slippers." (I'd just read *Little Women;* I could see myself bustling around in a hoop skirt.) "Freddy can go to Sewell and cheer up Grandpa. I'll stay home and take care of you."

Daddy sighed. "You're a dear for wanting to help me, but I can take care of myself. It's Freddy who'll need you in Sewell. Edith has a lot to do now. She is very serious and conscientious, and she doesn't know how to play with children the way Grandma did. Sometimes — Mama thinks — she is a little too strict, as though she were still in the classroom. Mama wants you to go to Sewell, not to protect Freddy from Edith — not exactly that — but so he won't be unhappy or homesick. You've got to be Grandma and Mama and me for Freddy. It's a lot to ask of you, but we think you can do it, and it's important for Mama and Freddy both."

I had been flattered by my parents' high opinion of me, and exhilarated by the prospect of telling Aunt Edith off when she needed it. I had agreed to go to Sewell with Freddy, but now, as the train jogged on and it occurred to me that already Aunt Edith was stepping into the automobile of whichever lucky beau she had chosen to drive her to the station to meet us, my courage began to ebb.

How beautiful Aunt Edith was — like Pola Negri — and clever and learned, and, for all her strictness — I had to admit — reasonable and fair! How I wished I looked like her instead of being a skinny dirty blonde, with a pug nose and freckles and size eight shoes! How I wished I could pay attention in school and get good marks instead of going off into daydreams! Neither would I have minded being followed around, like her, by a string of admiring beaus who thought I was wonderful even when I was mean to them! Most of all, though, I wished my dear, plump grandma, who always thought *I* was wonderful, was meeting me at Sewell Station as she always had done before. I wiped away a tear that had dribbled out of my eye. Freddy needed me, I told myself. Freddy loved me. Freddy thought I was pretty wonderful, and I had to keep cheerful so I could protect him from Aunt Edith. Resolutely I turned my thoughts to cheerful things about Sewell, and Haskell's Hill, and The Haven — which was the name of my grandparents' house — things that would be the way they had always been, even though Grandma was gone.

At the foot of Haskell's Hill, for instance, was Haskell's Cove. At low tide, it was more mud than water (though the channel was always deep) and loaded with clams. Freddy and I would put on bathing suits and old sneakers, get the clam hooks and the clam basket from the shed, and follow our secret path down to the cove. Our secret path was one Great-Grand-father Haskell had used when he ran his shipyard at the cove. The arborvitae hedge he had planted to screen the house and garden from the east wind had grown up into a miniature forest. You would never guess there used to be an opening in it and a gate, but once you had crawled through, you could trace Great-Grandfather's path zigzagging down through wild rosebushes, bayberry, sweet fern, and some stray arborvitae trees. In June and July, the rosebushes were all pink with blossoms and, as we brushed through them, a cool, lemony fragrance rose all around us. If we bent down, though, where our feet had crushed grass and sweet fern and bayberry, the smells were warm and dry and spicy. At the bottom of the hill, at low tide, the smell of mud rose up and overwhelmed all the other smells. Freddy and I — very knowledgeable because Bron had taught us — pounced on the likeliest-looking clam squirts, scraped out craters with our clam rakes, then, very carefully so as not to break the clams, probed down with our hands and lifted them out. We washed our catch standing knee-deep in mud at the channel's edge and usually, before starting home, had a mud fight, just for fun. Back at The Haven, we would stand at the door to the side porch and shout to Grandma to come see the surprise we had for her. She would appear suddenly out from under the big old wisteria that covered the side porch (the reason it was so big was because Grandma and her mother before her had always watered it with the dishwater) and she would throw up her hands in horror at the mud we had all over us, but she wasn't really angry. She'd get out the hose, chase after us, and squirt us until we were clean; then we would wash the clams, and she would steam them for lunch. She always said they were the best clams she had ever eaten.

It was impossible to remember anything pleasant about The Haven that didn't include Grandma. I hastily returned my thoughts to the cove. At half tide, from the top of the secret path, you could see how the North River wound in from Sewell Harbor through a waste of marsh to the foot of our hill. There it widened out into the cove. Narrowing again, it turned north and, still skirting the east side of the hill, it divided into branches which divided again and again and sent a network of tidal brooks into the marsh which stretched away to the north as well as the east and, in fact, surrounded Haskell's Hill on the west side too. At full tide, the river and its little branches flooded the marsh, and Haskell's Hill became a real peninsula. The narrow strip of land on which Haskell Street, coming from the town proper, ran past and a little above the cove was all that connected us, up on the hill, to the rest of Sewell.

High tide was swimming time at the cove. We had a diving raft in the channel. My father had built it when he was a boy, and Bron kept it in repair and put it out each summer for Freddy and me. Swimming and diving were one thing I was better at than Aunt Edith. It seemed funny to me that, growing up near the water, she didn't love it the way I did. I took to the water like a fish. How I soared through the air in my swans and jackknives! Like a bird, I saw the whole landscape spread beneath me and, when I came down, my head clove the water as neatly as a kingfisher's. My back dives, though, needed practice. I was always walloping the water with my shoulders and the tender part of my legs under the knee. It hurt like anything. I made an awfully big splash, too. The raft and our catboat, and even Bron's boat which was twenty-eight feet long, pitched like crazy, and the waves slapped against the beach.

If Bron was in his boat and gave me permission, I often swam over and climbed aboard to sunbathe on the forward deck. Bron's was a lobster boat that he had bought cheap because she was damaged. He had repaired and improved her so that he could live aboard in the summer and make money taking out summer people for fishing or excursions. He had fixed up the forward cabin with a bunk and a table, and a little sink and stove and icebox. Grandma had sewed him tiny yellow curtains that you could pull over the two portholes. He'd built a wheelhouse just aft of the cabin with a glass windshield and side windows, so he could run the boat in any weather and not get wet. Just last summer he had bought a beautiful mariners' compass and had it set in a mahogany counter just beside the wheel. He had wired the boat himself and polished up and electrified two old brass riding lamps and installed them port and starboard. Aft of the wheelhouse was a roomy cockpit with benches around for people to sit on. The big, new, silent Liberty motor stood in a mahogany box in the center of the cockpit. Bron had named his boat *Irene* after his mother, and I was disappointed that he hadn't named her after me and my grandmother and her grandmother and another beautiful ship of long ago.

I leaned my head against the back of my seat in the train and shut my eyes, the better to picture the ship *Jerusha*. Great-Grandfather Haskell had built her at his shipyard in the cove, and she had sailed from Sewell to Hong Kong on her maiden voyage in 1852. She was one of the fastest ships of her time and for twenty years, in spite of the competition of steamships, she made money in the China trade. I knew how beautiful she had been, for there were paintings of her in almost every room at The Haven.

On foggy days I liked to slip down to the cove alone just to imagine how the *Jerusha* had looked after her launching, waiting there in the cove to be fitted and to sail off to Hong Kong. Fog blotted out the familiar shapes of the two boats and the rafts, and the emptiness too. My imagination supplied the *Jerusha* and all the wharves and buildings and the bustle of Great-Grandfather Haskell's shipyard. Oxcarts unloaded planks and ropes and hardware on the big wharf. (At low tide you could still find a few stumps of the old piling in the mud.) A blind, white horse turned the capstan. The rasping of saws and the banging of hammers mingled with the stampings of oxen and the rumblings of their carts and the shouts of the drivers outside. Above all the noise, Great-Grandfather could always be heard bawling out orders. Huge, aloof, and silent, her masts towering as high as Haskell's Hill, the *Jerusha* floated, miraculously it seemed to me, in the narrow channel of the cove.

She had been launched on the full-moon spring tide, and, even so, had very nearly stuck fast. Everyone in Sewell had come to watch. Bets had been placed that so large a ship couldn't be launched in so small a body of water, but Great-Grandfather Haskell had done it. He had just given up seafaring to take over the shipyard from his father, who had sent him off at the age of thirteen as a cabin boy on a Haskell-built ship. He had become a captain before he was forty, and it was only because of his father's failing health that he left the sea. The *Jerusha* was one of the first ships built at the shipyard under his management.

His luck and hers ran high, and ran out together. The *Jerusha* was wrecked off Java. Orders at the shipyard got fewer. Henry Hardin robbed the safe, and that was the last straw. At the cove the wharves and buildings rotted, while up at the house Great-Grandfather raged to no purpose, Great-Grandmother whined and declined, and my dear, plump Grandma, young and slender then and almost pretty, sulked in her room and pieced a quilt ugly as sin.

She had told me about the quilt just last summer and had got it and shaken it out to show me and to air it. It was a crazy quilt and reminded me of thunderclouds slashed with lightning. It was so ugly it frightened me, and I guess it frightened Grandma too because she said (I remembered her exact words because they were so different from the sort of thing she usually said), "I must look at it sometimes to remind myself of my sin from which there is no escape." She folded it and laid it on the beautiful sunshine-and-shadow-pattern quilt we'd just smoothed over my bed. It crouched there like a toad. Ugh.

I didn't want to think about that quilt or my dear grandma who wasn't waiting at the station this year to hug me. I jerked my head forward, thumped my feet on the floor, and opened my eyes. We were slowing down for Sewell Station.

Opposite me, Freddy's face was almost hidden behind a huge, livid balloon of gum.

"Good for you," I said. "You've really got it, but we're almost there." The train braked suddenly, the balloon, with Freddy's head behind it, lurched right into my face. The lower half of Freddy sprawled in my lap.

"Sewell! End of the line," called the conductor.

Freddy scrambled to his feet. A strand of gum, firmly attached at one end to his mouth and at the other to the collar of my dress, stretched between us, divided into little threads which swung back and forth until they broke and attached themselves to Freddy's shirt front or the bodice of my dress. We tried to brush them away. They stuck to our hands, stretched some more, swung some more, broke, and hitched on to our chins, our noses, our eyebrows, and our hair. I looked at Freddy. He was a mess.

"Oh, Freddy, what will she say?"

Freddy's eyes widened; he began to giggle. He clapped his hand over his mouth to suppress the giggles, and his hand stuck there. I helped him pull his hand loose, and we were all stuck together again. The trellis of pink rambler roses behind the

station platform slipped by, then the station itself. Our train jerked and spluttered and dragged to a stop. There right under our window stood Aunt Edith. A man was pinning one of the pink rambler roses onto her white dress. Was it, perhaps, Bron? Hope swelled momentarily. The man turned. He was not Bron. He and Aunt Edith saw us and waved. Freddy and I wrenched ourselves apart.

"I'll go first." Freddy squared his shoulders. "It's my fault."

"No." With a sweeping gesture and trailing strings of gum, I swung down the suitcase and gestured Freddy behind me. "Come on." I started down the aisle.

"Your pocketbook!" Freddy snatched it from under the seat and handed it to me. We both stuck to it. We descended the coach steps awkwardly, held together by the pocketbook. Aunt Edith came forward, smiling. As her arms enfolded us, I felt the familiar hot gush from my nose. Aunt Edith checked her embrace.

"Dick," she cried, "Dick! She's bleeding!"

"It's one of her nosebleeds," said Freddy, tearing himself loose from me and jumping aside. "She often gets them. She can't help it."

"Nothing to worry about, Edith dear, though she's spoiled your dress," said Edith's beau. "Now, Jerry, don't you worry. Dr. Davis is looking after you. Just tilt back your head." A handkerchief was wadded under my nose. I was picked up bodily and deposited in Dr. Davis' flivver.

I will spare myself the embarrassment (which I still remember after eighteen years) of the further events of that evening. It is enough to say that Grandpa, hastening out of the side door of The Haven to meet us, mistook me for my mother in the throes of a hemorrhage of the lungs.

Edith's Narrative

Post Factum Introduction, November 1944

IT IS LIKE JERUSHA to plunge into her narrative as if she were plunging into the cove for a swim. I wish I had half her imagination and half her ability to bring memory to life in words. I am a pedestrian person with an orderly mind. I cannot launch myself on an undertaking as complicated as the joint writing of a memoir without first taking thought and planning ahead. Neither can I let Jerusha go off, as my high school students say, halfcocked. Before we proceed any further with our reminiscing, I am setting down here, for my own guidance and the enlightenment of any readers we may have: 1) who Jerusha and I are; 2) why and in what circumstances we are writing a reminiscence of the summer of 1926; 3) the method we propose to use; and 4) the result we hope to achieve.

Jerusha, who is as good-natured as she is impulsive, is not annoyed with me for interrupting her story. On the contrary, she says she is grateful to me for getting our project organized. I will proceed, then, with my delayed introduction. First I must explain who I am. My name is Edith Faunce. I am middle-aged and single. I have lived all my life in this house on Haskell Hill in the town of Sewell, Massachusetts, and I intend to die in it. My maternal grandfather, Captain Gamaliel Haskell, built the house, with the stable and outbuildings, in 1870 and named it The Haven. At that time, Grandfather was still a rich man. He spared no expense. The Haven was exactly as he wanted it and the showplace of Sewell.

The house has only two stories, like the cottage in which Grandfather grew up, but it has a mansard roof and a cupola. So does the stable. So do the hen house and the tool shed. Each of the posts in the fence which separates the formal yard from the road has its own cupola just like the one on the house, only smaller. Atop the cupolas on the house and barn, and on each of the four corners of their mansards, and on the gable end of the shed, there are iron lightning rods embellished with scrollwork and copper balls. The hen house, tool shed, and, naturally, the fence posts were considered too humble for lightning rods as either decoration or protection.

The formal yard within the fence is bisected by a gravel drive which passes the side door of the house (the one we always use) and continues back to the stable. The yard directly in front of the house is bisected in turn by a front walk made of marble slabs. In Grandfather's time flower beds, changed every season but always red, white, and blue, bordered the walk. The flower beds had gone to grass long before I can remember, and now many of the marble slabs are sunken and grown over. We never open the front door except during spring cleaning, or to make a draft through the house in summer.

The chief feature of the side yard is the flagpole, topped by a clipper ship for a weather vane, and circled, at the base, by another flower bed which originally spelled out HAVEN in red and white begonias and blue Vinca, but which I now plant each year in red, white, and blue petunias.

There are no large trees in the yard. Grandfather liked to be able to look up at the stars as he had been accustomed to do when he was at sea. An arborvitae hedge, grown to an untidy thicket, protects the house from the east wind off the sea, and a big, old wisteria vine covers the side porch and shields us from the summer sun. The house, the outbuildings, the fence posts, and all the cupolas have always been painted apple green. The trim around the doors and windows is white, and the doors and shutters are dark green. My grandfather chose these colors, and I have seen no reason to change them.

I know that according to modern notions The Haven is neither beautiful nor even very comfortable. Before the war, summer people used to drive up here just to make fun of it. They parked their cars right in front where I could hear them laughing. Father was never able to say boo to a sheep, and I tried to keep calm and ignore them, but sometimes they were just too aggravating. I would march out and tell them that they were parked on my private road which went on to the two Cornish cottages and nowhere else and, unless they had come to see me, or Mrs. Cornish, or whoever the tenants of her second cottage were, they were trespassing. They usually looked sheepish and pretended they were lost.

Friends tell me that in a few more years taste in architecture will change again and my house will be back in style and much admired. They mean well, but they neither reassure nor comfort me. On the contrary. I feel as if they were telling me that

I am out of style but that if I will just wait around a little longer I may be presentable again.

The Haven is much more than a house to me. It is my inheritance from my forebears, and all my life it has lived in me just as much as I have lived in it. We have been inseparable for so long that, at this late date, I could not survive a separation. We must go on together until I die, and after my death The Haven will still go on — not entirely without me. I have left it in my will jointly to Jerusha Spencer, née Faunce, and Frederick Faunce, the children of my deceased brother and sister-in-law, Haskell and Rose Faunce. I know that Jerusha and Freddy will keep The Haven in the family for my sake. They know that I consider The Haven to be the only part of me that is worthy to outlive me. (I have no illusions about the importance of my teaching career.) No wonder that I cannot stand to have The Haven laughed at, and that I am not grateful when I am told to make the best of it, as if it were a liability instead of my most valued possession.

The war, for all its misery, has rid me of nosy summer people and tactless friends. No one can get enough gas to drive way up here. Strangely enough, the war has also brought me an unexpected and undeserved happiness. My niece, Jerusha, and her two little boys are staying here at my invitation until they can go back to London. Jerusha was always impulsive, and it was just like her to go off and marry an Englishman. Not that I have anything against William Spencer. He is a doctor, and I can tell that Jerusha loves him. I know he is a considerate and thoughtful young man, for, in addition to writing to Jerusha, he writes me long and interesting letters about the army hospital in North Africa where he is stationed. I have to laugh at myself now, when I remember how I worried that

Jerusha and the children might upset Father and break the furniture and interfere with my schedule at school. The boys are darlings, bright as buttons, but gentle and loving. They remind me of Freddy when he was their age.

Having Jerusha here again has been such a joy to me. I guess I was lonely before she came though, heaven knows, I had Father and friends — not all of them tactless — and the whole of Sewell High School (I've been principal as well as Latin and history teacher for the past three years) to keep me busy. I can talk to Jerusha, though, as I can to no one else, about my feelings and about our family and the things that happened here long ago. She shares my love for Freddy, and she is the only person who understands about Bron Zebra. How I wish Haskell and Rose might have lived to see Freddy now and share our pride in him! Although he is still in his twenties, he is a lieutenant in the navy, stationed in the Pacific. He can't tell us where. Bron Zebra is no relative of ours, but once he was a very close friend.

When supper is over, the children asleep, the war news listened to and turned off, and Father reassured and settled for the night, Jerusha and I draw close to the fire in the parlor fireplace and talk. The war news, especially in the early days of Jerusha's visit, was not so reassuring as we tried to make Father believe, and it was partly to forget our anxiety for Freddy and William that Jerusha and I talked about the past. Soon the past — our past, inherited from shared ancestors and remembered from shared experience — took hold of us both and became the focus of our wartime life together.

In making repairs and improvements on The Haven or replacing its furnishings, I have taken pains to alter it as little as possible, inside as well as out. In the firelight, our parlor now, in 1944, looks much as it did in 1870 or 1912 or 1926. The low-ered shades (we have to do a brown-out all along the coast) and the stillness outside sharpen the feeling Jerusha and I both have that the parlor has become detached from time, that here the past and the present are happening all at once, and that there is no future. We exchange memories and impressions of events long past and people long dead, as if the events were happening around us and the people were with us. We tell each other stories we have heard from parents, grandparents, and old-timers, as if we were those personages and had been there our-selves. The more we talk, the more we remember, and the more we remember, the more we are drawn into and caught up by the summer of 1926. What a summer that was!

We were not yet recovered from Mother's death, and then in June we found the crazy quilt. It was a freak, a monster. Jerusha and Freddy were frightened. I was appalled, but Bron was intrigued by the anomaly. He studied it, and in September he found the key and deciphered the meaning. It was not a meaning we were happy to know. It did explain some things that had puzzled us, but the explanation was so unpalatable that Jerusha and I — the only ones besides Bron who knew it — agreed never to speak of it. Heaven knows how Bron felt about his discovery, or whether he has talked about it. His behavior, during that summer, was a greater anomaly than the crazy quilt, and he never explained himself. So much hap-pened in those few months! Events pile up in our memories until the crazy quilt is buried in the jumble. Jerusha and I have talked and talked, trying to make sense of it all. It is as vivid to us now as when it was going on, and as baffling. It is chiefly Bron — I might as well admit it — who fascinates and baffles us.

Last night while we were talking, one of the children cried

out upstairs. Jerusha jumped to her feet, then sat down and rested her head in her hands. When, a moment later, she got up again, she said, "I was lying in the sun on the forward deck of *Irene* with Freddy and Bron. We were drinking sarsaparilla and talking about our futures. Coming back from so far to now and the children made me dizzy."

Jerusha has always been able to dive, head-on, into imaginary situations and swim around in them like a fish. She is as much at home in a world of fancy as in the real world. I have very little imagination, but I understood what she meant. I too had been absorbed in my own memories of the summer of 1926.

While she was upstairs, Jerusha had one of her impulses. "Why not," she cried as she came down, "put in writing everything we remember about that summer? Bron," she went on, "studied the crazy quilt until he found the pattern in it. So must we study the events of that summer." Jerusha admitted that neither one of us had the quickness of mind and powers of concentration that Bron had, and for that very reason, we must write everything down. Writing about what had happened would demand more exactness and consequently more concentration than talking about it. If we wrote down our memories, leaving nothing out — not even the disagreeable business of the quilt — and if we disciplined ourselves to be honest at all costs and spare ourselves nothing, we might, just as Bron had, discover connections and interpretations that had never occurred to us before. We would be using Bron's method on Bron.

Jerusha's impulse intrigued me. We discussed it until well past our usual bedtime. We agreed that I should be responsible for writing the events which led up to the summer, since I had experienced them. From there on, we were on our own. Each of us would describe, in the fullest possible detail, the summer as she remembered it. When we had finished, we would edit our manuscript and cut out repetitions. We cannot be sure what we will come out with. It may be even more confusing and incoherent than our talks. However, we hope a pattern will emerge.

If we finish our reminiscence, Freddy, and Jerusha's boys when they are older, will want to read it, and they should. I believe it is best for Father to know nothing about it. At this late date, there is no need to distress him with the story of that crazy quilt. I burned it years ago. Neither would it make him happy to learn some other things that have been kept from him.

Background

At two-thirty in the afternoon on March 5, 1926, I was hearing my Virgil class recite at the Girls' Latin School in Boston, when a message came from the office that I had a long-distance call. It was from Dick Davis in Sewell. Mother had had a stroke. Dick told me not to worry. He would stay with her and Father until I could get home. Mother was as comfortable as could be expected and there was not much to do for her except get her to a hospital, and for that he needed my permission. Father didn't seem to understand. I said I could just catch the 3:58 out of South Station to Houghton Junction, and from there I'd get the 5:32 for Sewell. I asked Dick to have someone meet me at Sewell at 6:15. The principal was most kind. She took over my class and let me use her private phone to telephone Bron in Cambridge. Luckily Bron was in his room. He said he would meet me on the platform at South Station.

Bron hadn't brought any bag with him, but he had brought some books and, as soon as we had greeted each other and settled ourselves in the nonsmoking coach, he opened one of them — it was in Russian — and began to read.

Bron, at that time, was a graduate student at Harvard, working in Slavic languages and literature. He often invited me to Cambridge to listen to lectures he thought were especially interesting, and afterward over lunch or tea or supper, he would talk excitedly about the books he was reading or the paper he was writing. He was so enthusiastic that I loved listening to him, even when I didn't understand what he was talking about. In the midst of his talk, he would suddenly declare that I must do something impossible (for me) such as starting Russian immediately (Bron would lend me a book) so that we could read Pushkin together and I could have the same wonderful feeling Bron had for the poetry.

Just the summer before, he had been studying German to pass a language requirement. He had been all excited about some modern German writers and delivered passionate lectures to me — in German, too. He wanted me to study German with him, so we could read together. He said German was an easy language. I would pick it up in no time. I did study with him, and I think he thought the reason I didn't pick up German as quickly as he had expected was because I didn't really care. He could never understand that I just wasn't as clever as he was and wasn't cut out to be a scholar. At least I was clever enough to realize it. I had got an M.A. in Classics so I could teach in first-rate high schools. I enjoyed my teaching, and I enjoyed being able to use some of my salary for keeping up The Haven as it was meant to be.

Father was the Congregational minister in Sewell. His salary was tiny, and both his heart and his head were soft as butter. He was an easy touch for any no-account down on his luck. The fellow didn't even have to be a Congregationalist. My daydreams were not about reading Pushkin in Russian. They were about lifting myself and my parents out of our genteel poverty to the wealth and importance that our family had once enjoyed. I wanted us to be able to hold our heads as high as anyone in Sewell, and that included the rich summer people. When I married, I intended to be very particular. None of my beaus, though they were nice enough and very devoted, were at all what I had in mind. Not even Dick, though he was a good doctor and more devoted than anyone, came up to my idea of scratch.

Suddenly, full of guilt, I remembered how, for my sake, Dick was staying with Mother and Father now. I felt a surge of pity for Father, so good and so helpless, and for my dear mother, who had always looked after him and the whole parish too. What would become of them? Would Mother be an invalid? What if she died? Impossible. I couldn't imagine life without her. I tried to remember what Dick had said about her. He had been vague. Was that so as not to alarm me? I felt I would go crazy just sitting while the train bumbled along. I wished I had brought a book, like Bron, but I never would have been able to lose myself in a book at a time like this. That was another of the gifts Bron had which I had not.

I looked over at him. He wasn't reading at all. He was staring at the book while tears poured down his cheeks and splattered on the open page. I patted his shoulder and reached my handkerchief out of my bag and handed it to him.

"Don't cry, dear. You'll wear yourself out before we get there, and we won't be able to help Mother and Father as we should."

Bron took the handkerchief, blew his nose, then sobbed aloud.

"Please, Bron," I said. "Try to control yourself."

"I can't. I don't want to." Bron sobbed again.

"You're being childish." I patted his hand. "Mother needs sensible help, not tears."

"I love her. She has been a second mother to me," returned Bron in what seemed to me an unnecessarily loud voice, then choked and sobbed again.

"Hush, Bron." I squeezed his hand.

Bron pulled his hand away. "How can you sit there dry-eyed?" His voice rose louder than ever. "Don't you Yankees have any feelings?"

"Hush! People are listening."

"Let them," returned Bron. He blew his nose again.

"Don't make a scene, Bron."

"Do you love your mother?"

"What a stupid question, and a rude one, too." I was getting angry.

"You don't," retorted Bron. "If you did, you wouldn't care if a lot of strangers heard you crying."

"I am a grown woman. I try to think how I can help my mother when she needs help. I don't shout and bawl like a spoiled baby. How dare you say I don't love my own mother? She's *my* mother, not yours. You don't know anything about how I feel." I realized that my voice was rising and that I too was on the verge of tears. We hadn't had a fight like this in years. I stopped myself, but I couldn't help adding quietly, but with some annoyance, "You're different. You don't understand us, so please be quiet."

Bron gave his nose a final, indignant blow, wiped his eyes, and pocketed my handkerchief. "You are ashamed of me. Not only now, here in the train, but always."

His blue eyes were still moist and a little pink around the edges, but his jaw was set in a way I had never noticed before.

"Please, Bron. I don't want to talk."

"Bah!" said Bron. "You gave yourself away with that 'you don't understand us'! Why can't you say it out, honestly, that I'm Bron Zebra, the poor immigrant boy, and I've no right to cry for the mother of Miss Faunce of Sewell for though she is poor as a church mouse, she is beautiful and well-born, and a snob. Your mother is never like that. She sees people as they are in themselves and accepts them. She never cared who I was. She just loved me, and I have loved her almost as much as my own mother." Bron screened his eyes with the back of his hand.

Suddenly he changed his voice to an affected simper. "How humiliating for you, Miss Faunce! Your protégé — he owes everything to you and your family, and he really has done much better than anyone expected, considering his background — forgets his place, acts as if he were your equal, and in a public conveyance, too! It just goes to show you can't make a silk purse out of a sow's ear."

I had never been so spoken to, or so hurt, in my life. I stared at Bron with my mouth open. Then I felt tears coming, and turned quickly away to stare out the window and try to hold them back. I'd have died rather than let Bron see me cry.

After a long time Bron said, "I'm sorry."

I kept my voice steady long enough to say, "You should be."

Fortunately, the train was pulling into Houghton Junction. We had to shove our way out of the coach, dash across the tracks, and find seats on the Sewell local. When we were settled, I was able to say quite steadily, "If you really think I am the way you just described me, then, as soon as this crisis with Mother is over, we will stop having anything to do with each other. It must be very painful for you to be civil to me, let alone friendly."

Bron grabbed both my hands, and turned me sideways to face him. His eyes were full of tears, but he didn't sob or shout. "Forgive me," he said. "Don't leave me. You — you mean so much to me, and I can't tell you about it. When I try, I say it all wrong."

I wanted to tell him how hurt I was and how foolish he was to think I ever thought of him as my inferior, and yet perhaps I knew what he meant. Perhaps I did hold him off, in a way, as if he were an outsider, and exclude him from what was most important to me. "I forgive you," I said, "but I never thought. I never intended . . ." I couldn't go on. In my confusion and embarrassment I couldn't tell him anything.

He bent to kiss my hands. I noticed that his hair was very soft and blond — as it had been when he was a little boy. I remembered how I had touched it, in wonder at its softness and brightness, the first time I ever saw him, long ago.

Bron let go my hands, straightened, and turned away. Taking up that first memory of Bron, I dwelt on it and enlarged it to include the story of how Bron Zebra came to Sewell. It helped me, while we rode on, to forget my fears for Mother and the stiffness which, even though we had made up, I still felt between Bron and me.

The Zebras came to Sewell in 1907, on the same train on which Bron and I sat so uneasily together now. It was June when they came. Bron always said that his first memory of Sewell was the pink ramblers in bloom on the trellis behind the station platform, and shoving away one of the blossoms (although he really wanted it) which Mrs. Walker held out to him.

"Sewell Station," Mr. Walker, the conductor, called. "End of the line."

All the passengers got off except the Zebras. They sat tight — Mr. Zebra gripping the two suitcases, Mrs. Zebra hugging Bron and the bundle. Mr. Walker was worried about them. When he had punched the Zebras' tickets after they had come aboard at Houghton Junction, he had tried to ask them where they were planning to stay in Sewell. If anyone, he thought, as foreign-looking as the Zebras was coming to Sewell to visit or settle, the news would have been all over town. He suspected they had got on the wrong train. Mr. Zebra answered his questions with such a flood of gibberish and waving of arms that Mr. Walker retreated in confusion. Now, in Sewell, he was going to have to tackle Mr. Zebra again and persuade him somehow to leave the coach so it could be locked up for the night. The 6:15 always slept at Sewell and departed the next morning at 7:02. Mr. Walker knew now that with Mr. Zebra talk was useless. He pointed out the other passengers, who were either walking away from the station or being driven off in buggies and carryalls. (There were only two horseless carriages in Sewell in 1907.) Mr. Walker pantomimed listening — with his hand held to his ear — then, dropping his hand, he shuddered and jerked, at the same time emitting chugs and hisses which he gradually diminished in volume until, with a final *choo* and a shudder, he fell silent, closed his eyes, and pretended to be asleep. This was to tell the Zebras that, if they would listen, they would hear the engine letting off steam and settling down for the night. Bron told me later that he had enjoyed Mr. Walker's performance very much, although neither he nor his parents had understood it. Next, Mr. Walker pantomimed locking up the coach, driving home, eating supper, and finally lay down on a seat, tucked imaginary bedclothes around himself, and snored. Still puzzled, but believing that Mr. Walker meant them no ill, the Zebras finally made up their minds to file out with their luggage onto the platform. Once outside, Mr. Walker was able to take the Zebras up the platform, past the subsiding engine, and show them how the track stopped just beyond in a hay field. At last the Zebras understood. Mr. Zebra set down the suitcases and, waving his arms, launched into a tirade more terrible even than the one at Houghton Junction. Mrs. Zebra sat down on the bundle and wept. Bron threw himself howling on top of his mother.

All this time Mrs. Walker had been waiting patiently in the buggy to drive Mr. Walker home to supper. Mr. Walker turned to her for guidance. The Walkers agreed that they couldn't abandon the little family on the platform. They decided that they must persuade them to get into the buggy and then drive them up to Reverend Faunce's. Reverend Faunce had the world's softest heart, and Mrs. Faunce would know what to do next. Mrs. Walker drove the buggy alongside the Zebras and, with smiles and gestures, both Walkers invited the Zebras to climb in. It was during this operation that Bron refused the rose. Mr. Zebra watched the Walkers for some minutes before he decided to throw himself on their mercy. He loaded the suitcases and the bundle behind the seat, spoke to Mrs. Zebra and Bron, and helped them climb up. With a little bow and a gesture, he indicated that he would walk to save the horse. So, with Mr. Walker and Mr. Zebra walking beside the horse, Mrs. Walker drove Bron and his mother to our house.

My father and mother, my brother Haskell, and I were at supper in the kitchen when Haskell, whose chair faced the east bay window, jumped up. "Well I'll be —" he broke off to hold Mother and Father in suspense, expecting and fearing a blasphemy. He craned his neck to see around or through the wisteria. " — jiggered," he finished tamely. "Can I believe my eyes? I just saw a buggy turn into the drive with the old goosewoman and the little prince out of Edy's fairy story sitting up in the seat." He dropped his napkin and made for the hall and the side door. I jumped up and made after him.

The buggy had pulled up and there was Bron sitting in his mother's lap and smiling. The ride behind the horse had cheered him up. The sun, just about to dip behind our house, shone full on him, transforming his hair into a golden cloud. He did indeed look like the little prince in a fairy story. As Mr. Walker lifted him down, I reached out and touched his hair. I couldn't help it. I had to know how it felt.

So the Zebras came to Sewell and to us. We found out, in time, that their name was Zebrzycki. No one could pronounce it, so they were called Zebra for short. We also found out that they had immigrated from a small town in Poland, hoping to join relatives of uncertain name living somewhere in the northern United States. Soon after they landed in New York, Mr. Zebra had been tricked into giving away all his papers by a Polish-speaking crook who either needed them himself or sold them to someone else. Terrified of staying in New York, the Zebras took a train north because they knew their relatives lived in that direction. A series of mischances landed them in Sewell. By the time word came from the immigration authorities that we must either ship them back to Poland or be responsible for them here, they had become a part of our lives.

Mr. Zebra partitioned off the half of the stable that wasn't occupied by Buster, our horse, and made a comfortable apartment for his family. He also took care of Buster and the vegetable garden, fixed the leak in the kitchen roof, mowed the grass, tended the flower beds, and pruned the arborvitae and wisteria. In no time, he had our place (even though the buildings always needed paint) looking sprucer than it had since Grandfather Haskell's day. Mother found places for Mrs. Zebra to work by the day. She scrubbed things clean enough to satisfy the most particular housewives in the parish. Bron learned English so quickly and so well that Mr. and Mrs. Zebra, relying on him, never learned it at all. If they had learned to speak, or if there had been a Catholic church nearer than Houghton Landing, they might have mixed with the local people and made some friends.

When they died, Bron was particularly distressed because he hadn't somehow, by water if not by land, got them to church more than once or twice a year. I felt guilty too when the Zebras died. When I was a child, Mrs. Zebra had made effusively friendly overtures to me. Her effusiveness and her strangeness (she didn't even smell like other women) put me off. When I was older, though, I should have tried to learn a little Polish and talk to her about Bron and all his successes in school. They must often have been lonely and homesick, but on the whole, I think the Zebras were better off with us in Sewell than they were likely to have been anywhere else in this country.

They died within a few days of each other in the flu epidemic of 1919. Bron was away at college. They did not understand old Dr. Davis' order to stay in bed. They went to work as usual, developed pneumonia, and died. Bron spent far too much of his little inheritance on a fancy gravestone in the Catholic cemetery at Houghton Landing and on masses for their souls. I tried to persuade him that his parents would have preferred to have him use the money to continue his education, but he was stubborn, and Mother took his side.

As I looked at Bron, sitting tight-lipped on the seat beside me — he had put away his book — I had to admit that, for all his extravagant gestures, he managed his affairs well. He had all the clothes and books he needed, he paid his tuition charges and his rent, and without neglecting his studies to earn money, he had bought that boat, *Irene*. I couldn't see how he made enough by taking out summer people to pay expenses, let alone fix her up the way he had. However, that was none of my business. I must be careful, I told myself, not to add envy to the other blemishes on my character.

Bron turned to me and seemed to ask forgiveness with his smile. I smiled back. He reached out timidly and took my hand. I squeezed his, and we rode on, still not speaking, but in a friendlier mood with our joined hands lying on the seat between us.

So we had sat, our hands joined on the double bench, all

through Bron's first week at Sewell Harbor Primary School. I still remember how Miss Gerrish said she relied on me, a big third grader, to show Bron the ropes and help him with his letters. She told Mother later, with me standing right there listening, that without me Bron would never have got over his foreign ways so quickly or learned his letters so well. I almost burst with pride because right from the minute I first had seen Bron and touched his hair, I had felt that he was a kind fairy's gift to me. My brother was ten years older than I, and no families with children lived near us. A playmate, preferably younger, whom I could protect and teach and boss a little had been my dream, a dream so unlikely to come true that I hadn't even bothered to pray for it. Had I put in time praying, I'd have known that Bron was sent by the Lord, and a playmate of such exalted origin could not have filled my bill half so well. If I was bossy, Bron, once he had established himself, was stubborn. As children, we scrapped and made up over and over, but we were never bored with each other. When we weren't fighting (which often was rather fun) we thought up other interesting things to do.

While I was in high school, Mother let Bron do his homework with me in the parlor, although she wouldn't let any of my other friends. She said Bron and I were serious and ambitious and could help each other. Often, when we had finished our lessons, she would bring in a pot of cocoa and a plate of her sugar cookies (which Bron loved) and sit down to watch us eat and talk to us.

The decline of Sewell from the bustling seaport of her girlhood to a sleepy village saddened Mother, and the decline of Sewellians from captains and shipbuilders of renown to small shopkeepers, caretakers, chicken farmers, and jacks-of-all-trades dependent for their livelihood on gouging the summer people, mortified her. As a young girl, she had loved everything about shipyards and boats. She had kept her own catboat in the cove and often sailed in it to Houghton Landing for an afternoon's shopping. Though something of a tomboy for her generation, Mother also sewed fine seams and painted on glass as well as the other girls in Sewell, and she dutifully paid calls with her mother and helped her entertain at The Haven. Always, though, she was drawn by the boats and the business at the foot of the hill. Whenever she could, she would slip down to watch the carpenters at work or to listen, quiet as a mouse in a corner, to discussions in her father's office. She sensed, sooner than her father, that business was falling off, and she believed that slipshod management was one of the causes. She asked to be allowed to go to Houghton Junction to take a course in stenography and office management. Bron and I loved to have her act that scene out for us, as she took the parts, in turn, of her father, her mother, and herself.

The Haskells, father, mother, and daughter, sat in the parlor after supper. Mother and Grandmother were piecing a quilt of the oak-leaf design in green and white (I have it still). Grandfather was reading aloud from *Snarley-yow or The Dog Fiend* by Captain Marryat, his favorite author.

"Tomorrow," said Grandfather with an anticipatory chuckle, "we will read 'In which Mr. Vanslyperkin goes on shore to woo the widow Vandersloosh,'" and he reached for his night-cap of rum, lemon, sugar, and hot water which stood on the table beside him.

My mother put down her sewing. "Father." She sat very

straight and looked him in the eye: "A course in stenography and business management starts next Monday week at Miss Sparrow's Secretarial College at Houghton Junction."

"Indeed," said Grandfather Haskell.

"Yes," replied my mother, "and I have enrolled in the course. I have paid the registration fee, and I will pay the first term's tuition when I go to my first class a week from Monday. I sold three appliquéd quilts and an embroidered scarf to Grandma Davis who is blind and can't sew any longer. You will not be financially burdened."

"But they were for your hope chest!" cried out Grandmother Haskell.

"I'll have plenty of time to make more before I marry," replied Mother, tossing her head. "I'm in no hurry."

"Young lady," asked Grandfather, more puzzled than angry, "who put this idea in your head?"

"No one," replied Mother. "I read an advertisement in the *Houghton Register*. I sailed over to talk to Miss Sparrow who runs the school. She explained how I could learn to file papers, keep accounts, take dictation in shorthand, and type it all neatly with the new typewriting machine. I registered then, because I believe that with these skills I can be very useful to you at the shipyard. I shall go to school every morning on the seven-o-two train, which will get me to Houghton Junction at seven forty-five, in plenty of time for my first class at eight."

"No, no," cried Grandmother Haskell. "The train is too dangerous. It tips over. I beg you, Captain Haskell, forbid her to take the train."

"Be quiet, Mrs. Haskell. The train is irrelevant." Here Mother would scowl fiercely and somehow make herself swell until she looked very like the portrait of Grandfather Haskell which hangs in the dining room.

"Young lady, you will oblige me by never again speaking of the — er, accomplishments taught at that — er, establishment you so foolishly visited. The very words debase you. The accomplishments taught at that — er, establishment are for girls of the lowest classes as a last resort before . . ." He stopped short, drew a deep breath, and shouted, "I will never allow a daughter of mine to become a typewriter!"

Mother said she spent the next week working on her parents, persuading them to change their minds about the secretarial college. She explained to her father how she believed that modern business methods were needed to keep the shipyard from going under. She collected favorable opinions of Miss Sparrow and her college from Sewellians who knew Miss Sparrow or had heard of her undertaking. Finally, on a brisk September morning, she sailed both her parents to Houghton Landing to meet Miss Sparrow. Miss Sparrow proved to be not only a thorough lady, but a distant cousin of Grandmother Haskell. Grandfather Haskell was impressed by her air of authority. My mother was permitted to attend the college and ride the train. She only had to promise that she would practice her secretarial skills — once she had acquired them — in her father's business and nowhere else.

Mother went on to tell us that, with her keeping proper records and collecting bills promptly, and influencing her father to bend with the wind, the shipyard might have converted to building small pleasure boats and pulled through. The robbery, of course, finished everything. Mother never enlarged on it or on Henry Hardin, who did it. He had come up from New York for the summer to study the business. I've gathered from others that he was well recommended, well connected, and charming. Grandmother and Grandfather were delighted with him. They treated him like one of the family, and gossip has it that they hoped he would marry Mother. The safe he robbed was not the one in the office at the cove. It was the wall safe in what is now Father's study. It is still there, hidden behind the picture labeled *"Jerusha* in a gale off Hong Kong, 1866." Henry Hardin had abused his employers' hospitality to discover both the whereabouts of the safe and the combination. He also had learned somehow that on the day he robbed the safe, it would contain not only Grandfather's stock and bond certificates, the family jewelry, and the week's payroll for the shipyard, but $10,000 in gold bars that Grandfather was keeping for a few days for a friend. Nothing was ever recovered, and Henry Hardin was never heard of again.

Bron and I sometimes speculated about a romance between Henry Hardin and Mother, and once Bron was fresh enough to ask her pointblank if she hadn't been just a little sweet on Henry Hardin. Mother, usually so indulgent of Bron, froze him with a hard, blue stare and ordered him to bed. In the same way, I was sure, Grandfather Haskell had disposed of impertinence on his quarter-deck. Neither Bron nor I dared touch on the subject with her again. We agreed, though, that Mother very likely was taken in by Henry Hardin like everyone else. Since she always assured us that she hadn't been a beauty when she was young and had never had many beaus, we thought it likely she might even have fallen a little in love with the charming Henry.

She told us that after the robbery she had had a nervous breakdown and kept to her room for a whole year. Meanwhile her enraged father tried to find the thief, pay back his friend,

and restore his business and his credit in such a senseless rush
of activity that he gave himself a heart attack and died. Had
he lived longer, Mother said, he would have lost The Haven
and his land on Haskell's Hill, along with everything else.
His death forced Mother to come downstairs. She went to
work and supported her mother and herself by being a public
stenographer.

Let this be a warning, Mother admonished Bron and me
over the empty cocoa cups, never to indulge, as she had, in
self-pity. Determination to do our cheerful and unselfish best
in whatever work the Lord sent us would, according to
Mother, enable Bron and me to rise and shine as worthy Sewellians should. Mother proved her own point, for, no sooner
had she cast off self-pity than the Lord sent her her lifework
in the form of Father. He had only been in Sewell two weeks
but already he was hopelessly behind in his paperwork. The
vestry hired her to take letters for him.

How Mother loved to tell about their first meeting. "He was
as handsome as a saint," she'd say, "and he had a voice like an
organ, and he was so good and so helpless. I knew right away
that he liked me because of the way he confided in me about
his shirt. It was frayed at the collar and cuffs and stained down
the front. He said he was sure it wasn't the same one he had
given Mrs. Acker to wash. That one had been quite new and
— he wasn't positive — he thought he had seen it on Mr. Acker
only the day before. He said Mrs. Acker was so efficient about
everything, he didn't see how she could have made such a
mistake, and he was a little afraid of her and hated to ask her."

Mother would chuckle as she described how she managed
Mrs. Acker. I believe she made up her mind to marry Father
at that first meeting.

The Death of My Mother

I FELT A TUG on my hand. Bron was standing up. The train slowed down as it approached Sewell Station. I put aside my memories and prepared to meet reality.

It was almost dark on the platform, and I didn't recognize Dick until he was taking my hand.

"You are good to come yourself," I said. "I hope that they — that everything . . ."

"How is she?" interrupted Bron. "How is Mrs. Faunce?"

"I didn't know you were here, too," said Dick. "I'll explain everything to Edith while we are driving to the house." He put his hand under my elbow to direct me to his car. "I suppose you'll want to drive up with us," he said over his shoulder to Bron.

"That's right," said Bron. He ran ahead and climbed into the back seat of Dick's Model T.

Dick settled me in front before he climbed into the driver's seat beside me. Leaning forward, Bron stuck his head between Dick and me.

"How is she? Is she conscious? I hope you aren't letting her suffer. What — what are her chances?"

I could tell by the way Dick banged his foot down on the starter that he was annoyed.

"Come, Bron," I said. "Don't rush him so, and you might thank him for coming to meet us, too." I laid my hand, soothingly I hoped, on Dick's arm and waited for Bron to say something polite and apologetic. Bron said nothing.

"Thank you, Edith," said Dick. He snapped on the headlights. The flivver trembled all over, made some preliminary lunges, and set off.

"How is Mrs. Faunce?" demanded Bron. He was literally breathing down our necks.

Dick ignored him. "I don't want to alarm you, Edith," he began in his best professional manner. "On the other hand, I must prepare you for a very serious situation at The Haven. She has come out of the coma, which is a good sign; however, there is complete hemiplegia of the right side — that is, paralysis — and vocal motor aphasia as well. She can't speak. However, partial recovery is by no means impossible. Good nursing will make all the difference. There is only one private nurse around now whom I would trust with the case, and she, of course, is busy. I strongly advised Reverend Faunce to send his wife to the hospital immediately. He begged me to let him nurse her because she would be so much happier at home with him." Dick sighed. "Of course Mr. Faunce can't nurse her, but it is impossible for me to make him understand. Edith, I know you will want to nurse her too, but you are not a trained nurse, and it would be professionally negligent of me to give you the responsibility in such a serious case, especially in this early, critical stage."

"I'll help you," put in Bron. "Together we can manage it. We'll do exactly as you tell us, and, you'll see, she'll get better much faster at home than she ever would in a hospital."

Dick said nothing, but again I knew he was annoyed, this time by the way he jerked the flivver around the corner from Station Avenue onto Haskell Street. Again I laid my hand on his arm.

"Edith," said Dick, "I hope you will instruct me now to

telephone for a room at the hospital and an ambulance to take your mother there. I will do it as soon as we get to The Haven. It is important. We can persuade your father of its importance later, and then, if your mother gets so she can move around a little, and there is less danger of pneumonia and kidney infection, perhaps she can come home. Now, I believe she should be in a hospital under expert care."

"Don't send her to a hospital, Edy," cried Bron into my ear. "She'll hate it. It will kill her. We can take care of her. I know we can."

Beside me I heard Dick swallow his anger. "It is up to you, Edith," he said.

"Please telephone as soon as we get home."

Dick took his hand from the wheel for a moment to press mine. "Good," he said. It was the words pneumonia and infection that made me decide for the hospital, and if Bron thought I was too cold-hearted and selfish to want to give up my time to nursing, I couldn't help it.

Dick went on to say that he had telephoned my brother Haskell in Chicago, and that he was coming as fast as he could. The flivver bumped off the section of Haskell Street that was maintained by the town; from here on, past the cove and up our hill, Dick gave all his attention to guiding it through the bumps and potholes of our private end of Haskell Street, which was not maintained at all. As we turned into our driveway, a shiver ran up my spine. Except for a single light glaring out from the unshaded window of Mother's bedroom, The Haven was dark. How different it looked, with lights cozily glowing through drawn shades, on ordinary Friday nights when Dick drove me home for the weekend. We entered through the side door, which was open and banging in a cold east wind. As we groped for the chain of the hall light, Sunbeam, Mother's old ginger cat, twined around our legs, mewing and nearly tripping up Dick, who swore under his breath. Bron found the light chain and we all blinked at each other. Sunbeam yowled indignantly and tried to shunt my feet toward the kitchen.

"I'll telephone now," said Dick. "The ambulance should be here in half an hour." He made for the phone in the dining room.

Bron scooped up Sunbeam. "Go up to see her, Edith. Tell her I'm feeding Sunbeam and will be right along, and try to look a little bit cheerful, and forgive me again for butting in."

I climbed the stairs and entered the bedroom.

Mother was propped up in bed in a half-sitting position. Father sat beside her, holding her crippled right hand. I bent over to kiss her but, as I looked in her face, my blood chilled. It was not her twisted mouth or the horrible sound which came from it that chilled me. It was the look in her eyes — a look of terror. I had seen my mother look many ways but never terrified. I mumbled, not cheerfully as I had intended, that Bron was downstairs, that Haskell was on his way from Chicago, that Dr. Davis recommended a few days in the hospital, and that the ambulance would arrive soon. With her good left hand Mother gripped mine. More incomprehensible sounds came from her twisted mouth. Her eyes bulged with the effort she was making. Exhausted, she let go my hand, sagged over sideways, and might have fallen out of the bed if Father and I hadn't caught her. We straightened her and tried to make her comfortable.

"No need to talk, dear," I said, kissing her again. "Bron and I are here to help Father, and Haskell is coming." She

made an impatient gesture with her left hand, and fixed her terrible eyes on me. I turned away from them to Father. "What does she want?" I asked him.

"I do not know," said Father. "She tries to speak and wears herself out." He bent low over Mother and smoothed her forehead. "There is nothing so important for you now, Jerusha my love, as rest. When the Lord means you to tell us what you have in your heart, be assured, He will find the way for you. Now let us pray quietly together. She understands" — he turned to me — "everything I say to her." His voice and the words of his prayer were gentle and comforting. I glanced again into Mother's eyes, hoping to see some sign of relief. The terror in them was unabated, and they seemed to bore into me, begging for help.

"Perhaps she can write what she wants to tell us with her left hand." As I said this, I thought I saw a flicker of hope in Mother's eyes. I fetched a pencil and a pad of paper. Father and I raised her shoulders a little. I put the pencil in her left hand and held the pad for her. With her hand shaking crazily, she scrawled a few words on the pad before she dropped the pencil.

Bron came in. As he bent over her, and she looked up at him, I saw him wince, then brace himself. He bent lower and kissed her and managed to look straight into her eyes and smile while he told her how much he loved her and how he was going to see to it that she got well. He and I, he said, had come expressly to take care of Father, while Mother spent a few days in the hospital. She must leave everything to us. We could handle Father, the house, the parish, anything. She must concentrate all her strength on getting well, and she would. Bron was sure of it. And to show how efficient he was, he told her that he had just fed Sunbeam, and here was the old fellow himself come to pay his respects and assure her that he (Sunbeam) had confidence in Bron.

Sunbeam had come in with Bron and sat down on the floor beside the bed to consider whether to jump up or not. At this moment he made up his mind, jumped onto the foot of Mother's bed and started on his postprandial wash-up. I hoped that Bron's pleasant chatter would reassure Mother, and that the visit from Sunbeam would amuse her. I waited for the terror to leave her eyes, but it stayed on.

I hastened to explain to Bron that Mother was trying to write a message to us, and I showed him the pad with her scrawl. He agreed with Father and me that the first word was *quilt*. Further along, we thought we could make out a *c* and an *sh,* but the other letters were so misshapen that no one of us could make anything of them.

"Let's get her the quilt now and have her try again on the other words when she has rested," whispered Bron. "Which quilt do you think she wants?"

"The clam-shell quilt in the guest room closet," I cried. I felt sure I was right. *C* and *sh* certainly fitted, and I knew that Mother set great store by her clam-shell quilt. The pattern, to be effective, demands great precision in measuring, cutting, and piecing. Mother's quilt was an especially handsome specimen — in blue and white — and had won several prizes. How like her, I thought, to want it now to perk her up when she was laid so low and to impress the strangers who would come into her room here and at the hospital. As I unwrapped the quilt and carried it to Mother's room, I smiled fondly to think how proud my mother was in her modest way, and how, for all she didn't judge others, she knew her own worth and took satisfaction in it.

I spread the quilt over her and Sunbeam too and expected to see the terror in her eyes give way to relief. She plucked at the quilt with her good hand as if to throw it off the bed. She made more unintelligible sounds. More desperately than ever her eyes implored us to understand and help. Finally she raised her good hand and shook it impatiently in the general direction of the door. During the next ten minutes, while Bron and Father anxiously watched, I brought in every quilt in the house and spread each one for Mother to see. She wanted none of them. I made a quick search of the loft over the kitchen ell, although I had myself, during my Christmas holiday, gone through everything there. I had thrown out the junk and repacked the trunks and boxes, labeling them "Old sermons," "Sewing scraps," "Photographs," "Clothes," and so on. There had been no quilts there then, and there weren't any now.

"Isn't there another storeroom under the mansard?" whispered Bron.

I shook my head.

"What about the trap door in the hall ceiling with the pull-up ladder that she never let us pull down? Doesn't it go to the cupola? Cupola begins with *c*."

Again I shook my head. "The windows are broken in the cupola, and it leaks, and the pigeons have taken it over. There's nothing there but pigeon nests. I've looked. She wouldn't store anything she valued there. Oh Bron, I don't know what to do."

"Let's let her try the writing again," said Bron. "I know it tires her" — he turned to Father — "but she wants to tell us something important. She won't be able to rest until she has."

We found the pencil under the bed. Bron helped Father to raise Mother while I put the pencil in her hand and held the pad for her. Her hand was more unsteady than ever, and what she wrote was quite impossible to read. We thought we could make out *up* and a *p* and an *i* — no more. Bron turned to Mother.

"We can't read this very well," he said. "We will guess at each word, and when we guess right, will you tap once with your hand? Do you understand?" Mother tapped once. Again I saw a ray of hope in her eyes.

I smiled at her. "We'll figure it out," I said. "You always said that Bron and I were serious and clever, and you were right."

"Up?" asked Bron.

Mother tapped.

"In?" asked Bron.

Mother tapped again.

"Closet?" I tried.

No tap.

"Shed?" I tried again.

No tap.

"Pipe?" interrupted Bron.

No tap.

"What is going on here?" Dick strode in.

"Leave us alone," said Bron. "We're trying to find out something."

At this moment Sunbeam, who was still under the latest quilt we had spread over Mother, came out for air, sprang from the foot of the bed onto Mother's pillow, settled himself, and resumed his washing.

"Good God!" cried Dick. "Are you insane, that you let dirty animals wash themselves on the pillow of a patient whose life depends on her not picking up an infection? What sort of nursing care is that?" He swept Sunbeam off the pillow. "Edith, I — I had expected better of *you*, at least."

"You don't understand," said Bron.

Dick's face flushed. "That's enough from you," he shouted. "I'm sorry, Edith and Mr. Faunce," he added after a moment, "but unless this — this Zebra leaves the room at once, along with the cat, I'm giving up this case."

I saw Bron clench his fists. I put my arm around him from behind and with all my strength shoved him ahead of me out the door. Sunbeam had left already. Dick shut the door behind us. A moment later I heard the ambulance turn into our driveway.

Father and I went with Mother and saw her settled in her room at the hospital. Dick asked us not to sit up with her, but to go home and sleep. He put her under sedation and assured us that she would rest quietly through the night. A special-duty nurse sat with her, and he himself slept at the hospital to be on instant call. I don't see how he could have done more. However, when the nurse was out of the room for a minute, Mother, who had seemed to be asleep, jerked herself sideways, got her left hand on a pencil lying on the bedside table, and then toppled half out of the bed and hit her head against the table leg. The nurse came back, got her back in bed, and called Dick, but Mother had had another stroke. This one was fatal.

Jerusha's Narrative

My First Morning

Waking was bliss on those long-ago summer mornings at The Haven. Smells of the marsh and the sea and the tang of arborvitae filtered into my sleep. Warm water, shot with sun shafts, washed over and around me and buoyed me up. Yet I was not wet, and I breathed freely. I skimmed the water like a boat, cruising among clouds of sea lavender and bushes bearing beach plums as big and shiny as eggplants. Like a fish I flicked through depths of luminous emerald, then, rising up and up, I burst into the glorious sunlight of the real day. Sunlight flashed from the glass of my mirror and from the painting above the glass of my own ship, the *Jerusha,* rounding Gull Point Light in a froth of foam. Sunbeams fingered the backs of the old-fashioned books in my bookcase, and set the golden Gothic lettering of their titles aglow. Sun flecks danced over the patchwork coverlet Grandma had made especially for me from scraps I picked myself. It was aptly named "Sunshine and shadow." "School is over," I would think, "and I'm at The Haven," and I would be filled with great peace and happiness.

My first waking at The Haven in the summer of 1926 was not typical, but at least it saved me the pain of emerging from bliss into the realization that Grandma was dead and that nothing at The Haven would be the same. I was wakened by jabs and shakes, and Freddy's voice saying, "Guess what, Jerry?" Thus Freddy woke me every morning of the school year, and I responded the way I did in Chicago.

I said, "What?" without opening my eyes, and settled back to steal a few more minutes of rest. At home Freddy would tell me how another speakeasy had been raided, or another gangster rubbed out, or the Cubs or Notre Dame had won another game. Freddy had a morning paper route. He woke the family as soon as he got back and informed us of important developments in the world.

"Auntie made waffles. I ate five."

I opened my eyes and took in my room and Freddy's face above me. I remembered everything.

"I bet her waffles aren't as good as Grandma's," I muttered.

"They're good," replied Freddy, "and she lets you have all the syrup you want. Real maple syrup." He belched.

I saw that his chin was glazed with syrup and his eyes glazed with the effort of digesting. "You ate too much."

"I know it." Freddy curled up on the foot of my bed. "I kept waiting for her to tell me to stop, or at least to say, 'Eat more slowly,' or 'Don't waste syrup,' but she never said anything. She let me put the batter in the waffle iron myself. It's a nifty new electric waffle iron. Chester gave it to her. If you put in too much batter, the lid rises up when the batter rises inside, and gobs of batter gush out and run down the sides. You can scrape them off with a knife and eat them while you're waiting for the waffle inside to get done. It's messy as anything, but she never said a word. Honest, Jerry, she's not so crabby as she used to be."

"She just likes you. Wait 'til I come down."

Freddy licked the fingers of his right hand one by one. "She's going to make fresh batter especially for you when you come down, and she told me not to wake you because you needed to sleep, but I did anyway."

"Thanks."

"Don't be sacristic, Jerry. I wanted to tell you about the waffles and my plan to dig clams."

I didn't bother to correct Freddy's pronunciation. I half sat up. "What's your plan?"

"The tide's dead low at nine thirty-six. The reason I woke you up is so we can go dig some clams in the cove and give them to Auntie and Grandpa for a surprise. If you get up now, you've got time to eat your waffles before we go. We'll see Bron at the cove, too. He's in his boat. Auntie says he must have taken out a fishing party last night because he didn't come to see us when we first got here, and he didn't come up for breakfast either, even though Auntie told him she was making waffles on the new iron. Bron loves waffles, so he must have overslept. We'll wake him up. Grandpa wants to see you to be sure you are all right and aren't Mama. I told him you were yourself and you often had nosebleeds, but he's still worried. He has a meeting with the officers of the Women's Alliance at ten. At nine-fifteen I'm to remind Auntie to remind him." Freddy drew a deep breath and let it out slowly. "I've got a lot to do, and I'm awfully full."

I considered all this and the sunlight that was dancing over Freddy and my quilt. Being grumpy didn't seem worth the trouble.

"I'd like to see Bron and dig some clams. I just hope Aunt Edith doesn't think up some old chore for us to do so we miss the tide."

"As a matter of fact," said Freddy, "before we go anywhere, we've got to write penny postcards to Mama and Daddy. Auntie's got them for us. She sent me upstairs to wash my hands so I wouldn't smear my postcards all up." Freddy sighed. "It's not that I don't want to write to Mama and Daddy. It's just that I'm so full."

I sat all the way up. "You can stay here and rest until I'm through in the bathroom. Then you wash, and you can write your postcards while I'm eating. It won't take me more than a minute to write mine. We'll get to the cove in plenty of time."

I jumped out of bed and tossed my pillow to Freddy. He caught it and belched again.

"Thanks, Jerry. I just need a few minutes to let them settle."

In the kitchen, sunlight poured through the big bay window and over the breakfast table with the new waffle iron standing in its center and Grandpa, Freddy, and Sunbeam seated around it. The waffle iron flashed silver. Sunbeam flashed gold. Freddy's brown hair shone like polished mahogany as he bent over his postcards, and Grandpa's thick, white curls formed an aureole around his handsome face. He was pouring cream into a saucer for Sunbeam, who sat up in a chair beside him. Sunbeam was keeping close track of the cream, but even so he saw me before anyone else did. He acknowledged and dismissed me with a flick of his yellow eyes before he sniffed the cream, tried it with his tongue to be sure it was fresh, and got down to business with it. Grandpa saw me next. He set down the pitcher and, rising to his full six foot two — he was neither stooped nor shrunken — came toward me with outstretched arms. After he had embraced me, he held me at arm's length to examine me. I smiled into his gentle brown eyes. They brimmed over with love, trust, and sadness, like the eyes of a spaniel who tries hard, means well, and is puzzled. Grandpa's eyes were at odds with his imposing height and apostolic head, but not with his voice.

"Yes, it is little Jerusha," he said with all the rich, melancholy vibrations of a violoncello. Grandma had once told me that, when he was a young man, the sound of his voice reading out the notices in church caused ladies to swoon even before the sermon began. I didn't swoon, but I was moved. I wanted to reassure him and make him happy.

"That's right, Grandpa," I said, "but I'm getting taller all the time. I grew an inch last year, and I got a Good Health Certificate from school because I was the only girl in the eighth grade who didn't miss a day."

"Good health is a great blessing. Your grandmama enjoyed good health until the end. She is greatly missed." He gave me a long, dismal look, patted my shoulders, and dropped his hands to his sides. "Last night, in the shadows," he went on, "I mistook you for your poor, sick mama. I am often confused these days. You must forgive me. Now, in the sunlight, I notice a resemblance between you and your dear grandmama."

"Mama says I look more like Grandma than anyone else in the family. She hopes that having me around this summer will remind you of Grandma in a happy way and cheer you up."

Grandpa considered carefully before he said, "Nothing cheers me up much, but it was kind of your mama to think of me. She is not well herself. I hope she is no worse than when we last heard from her."

"She's better," I said. "She's gained a pound and almost stopped coughing. Her doctor says that a summer in the mountains will make her all well again."

"Let us hope so," replied Grandpa. "I have always understood that it was sea air that was especially beneficial to weak lungs. My cousin Harriet Cornish is of the same opinion. She first came to Sewell from New York City to take the sea air. She has been coming now for fifteen years and enjoys robust health. I could wish your mama had come here too. These modern doctors are very cocksure, but you can't always trust them. The young Dr. Davis did not handle your grandmama's case at all well. If the old doctor, his father, had been alive to treat her, she might be with us still. I miss my dear wife sorely, little Jerusha, sorely."

"We all miss her, Grandpa," I said.

"Not so much as I do," replied Grandpa. From his pocket he drew an enormous, snowy handkerchief, wiped his eyes and nose, and returned the handkerchief to his pocket before going on more lugubriously than ever: "Since she died, nothing is right. Come sit down with me, little Jerusha, and I will tell you about it." He pulled out a chair for me as if I were a grown-up lady. I would have liked to take a minute to pat old Sunbeam and scratch his jowls for him, but I couldn't keep Grandpa waiting. I sat down. Grandpa drew his chair close to mine and fixing me with his puzzled eyes, began in a loud whisper.

"Edith is very clever and very kind. She takes care of me. She reminds me of my appointments, of names I forget, but she has a great many beaus. Every night young men come to see her or take her away in fast automobiles. She cannot sit with me after supper and discuss the day's doings as my dear wife used to do. Sometimes Bron comes to sit with me. We talk about my dear wife and his parents, and of the old days." Grandpa sighed. "It cheers me a little to talk with Bron, but of late he hardly ever comes. I cannot understand this." Grandpa's beautiful, puzzled eyes sought out mine. I could only shake my head to show that I didn't understand either. "My dear wife would have understood," Grandpa went on. "If she were here, she would set us all right again." Grandpa fetched a particularly loud and dismal sigh.

Sunbeam polished off the last of the cream, sat down, gave himself a few licks, and looked about vaguely. He was considering in his mind all the places where he might take his nap and trying to choose the one that suited him best. Grandpa understood. He moved his chair back a bit from the table and smoothed and patted his trousers to show Sunbeam that he'd be welcome in his lap. Sunbeam was not to be hurried. He went on considering.

Grandpa turned back to me. "I'm sure everyone means to be kind," he said, but not as though he really believed it. "One of Edith's beaus — I think it was the Bates boy — yes, I'm sure it was, because he brought the waffle iron, too, for Edith's birthday, and he was wearing his new uniform. The Bates boy brought me a radio. He taught me how to run it so I could listen to it at night when I was alone. It was very kind of him, but, oh, little Jerusha" — Grandpa leaned closer and spoke lower — "don't tell Edith, but I cannot bear the music that comes out of that radio. It has no tune, no harmony. It is just noise." Sunbeam finally made up his mind and transferred himself from his own chair to Grandpa's lap, where he settled down and commenced to purr. Grandpa stroked him and after listening carefully to his rumblings, announced, "The sounds that come out of this cat are more musical than the sounds that come out of that radio, and as for the news that comes out, that disturbs me even more than the so-called music." Grandpa's eyes widened with alarm. "What terrible things go on these days! Especially in Chicago! Oh, little Jerusha, when I hear of gangsters running loose in the streets, robbing and killing, I become so upset that I walk the floor until Edith comes in, and I beg her to telegraph Haskell to ask if you are still alive out there and to advise him to move his family away at once before you are all murdered. Edith does not understand how upset I am. She tells me there is nothing to worry about and to take a sleeping pill. Young Dr. Davis' sleeping pills are of no use. I think they keep me awake."

"You really shouldn't worry so about us, Grandpa. Chicago isn't nearly so bad as the news announcers make out. Where we live it is very quiet, almost like Boston. Hardly anyone ever gets robbed or shot."

"Now you sound like Edith, and you are both wrong. Every day your father must go to his office in the city. How can he not be in danger when, all around him, gangsters are racing from one speakeasy to another, shooting each other, and policemen are shooting at the gangsters. No, no, don't try to contradict me." Grandpa thumped his hand on the table, but this show of spirit seemed to tire him and leave him glummer than before. "The news is full of words I do not understand," he muttered. "I do not know what a speakeasy is."

I was glad to inform Grandpa. "Speakeasies are places where people can buy whiskey and wine and things like that." (I wasn't up on the names of alcoholic beverages.) "Since it's ille-gal now, with prohibition, to sell any kind of whiskey or what-ever, the speakeasies have to run secretly. If you want to buy a drink, you have to belong to a speakeasy the way you belong to a club. You have to say a password to get in." I felt I was doing well and went on. "The police raid the speakeasies every so often, just so they'll seem to be doing their duty. Actually the police are controlled by the big gangsters who run the speak-easies too, and just about everything else in Chicago. Daddy says that prohibition has done more harm than good. He says the only people it has stopped from drinking are the ones who never drank much anyway, and that because the prohibition can't be really enforced, it encourages people to break it, and that encourages corruption and graft and speakeasies and boot-leggers and rumrunners and gangsters and racketeers and gun molls and stool pigeons and . . ."

"That is enough, little Jerusha. That is enough." Grandpa raised his hand like an outraged apostle. "You young people are all alike," he went on petulantly. "You tell me not to worry and then go on to tell me that conditions in this sad world are far worse than I ever dreamed. Only a few days ago, another of Edith's beaus — he wore a uniform, too, but he wasn't the Bates boy. It wasn't a policeman's uniform. I believe it was a Coast Guard uniform, but I can't recall the fellow's name. This Coast Guard fellow told me that smugglers, rumrunners I be-lieve he called them, were bringing illegal liquor from Canada in boats and landing it right here in Sewell. He said the Coast Guard was running extra patrols to catch them and that if I heard shots in the night, I was not to be alarmed.

" 'My dear Lieutenant,' I said, 'how can you tell me not to be alarmed when I hear shots in the night? If a man hears shots in the night, and is not alarmed, he is lacking in judgment and common sense.'

"This lieutenant fellow said he thought I would be less alarmed if I knew what the shooting was about. I told him that, on the contrary, I would feel less alarmed if I didn't know that what I heard were shots at all. Then I could attribute the sounds to some harmless explosion." Grandfather shook his head at me. His eyes were more puzzled than ever. Suddenly tears sprang from them. "Oh, little Jerusha, I am very miserable, very miserable indeed!" He began to cry like a baby.

"Oh, Grandpa," I cried, "don't!" I couldn't think of anything else to say or do for him. I was paralyzed by my embarrassment. I thought Sunbeam must have been embarrassed, too. He jumped off Grandpa's lap and loped out the door.

Aunt Edith came in from the shed. "Father!" she cried. Like me, she was too embarrassed to go on.

Freddy looked up from his postcards and quite literally jumped to Grandpa's rescue. He hurtled into the old man's lap and smothered him with hugs and kisses and little cries of sympathy. He helped Grandpa find and unfurl his pocket handkerchief. Gently as a mother, he helped him to blow his nose and dry his tears. Finally he snuggled down comfortably in Grandpa's lap.

"This is a very dear child," said Grandpa, after gazing thoughtfully at Freddy. "My next Sunday's sermon will be about him. I think, Edith and little Jerusha, that you will not be ashamed of my sermon." He stroked Freddy's hair and gazed benignly through and beyond Aunt Edith and me as if he were already at work on the sermon.

I felt ashamed of myself for having been ashamed of Grandpa, and my heart went out to Freddy. What a swell little brother he was — never a showoff or sneaky like other little kids, but all open and loving the way the Bible says children are (but, except for Freddy, they aren't).

Aunt Edith drew a long breath, almost a sigh. I glanced up at her. With her smooth, dark hair piled high on her head (she never bobbed it), her regular features, high, clear color, and long neck — I believe it was the kind of neck that in poems is called swanlike — she could have been the beautiful girl on an old-fashioned candy box. Mostly I just envied her good looks and resented the rest of her. Now, as with a gentle, almost wistful smile, she looked down on Grandpa and Freddy, I realized that she was feeling just the way I did — ashamed of herself for being ashamed of Grandpa and full of love for Freddy, and gratitude too. So she couldn't be as stuck-up as I'd always believed she was.

My feeling of kinship with Aunt Edith lasted only a minute. She turned to me. "Good morning, Jerusha." Her smile had changed to brisk. "I hope you have had a good sleep. You must have been very tired after the long trip and all the responsibility. I must say that, for such a young girl, you managed the trip very well." She gave my shoulder a little pat. I went stiff.

"Always condescending," I thought, "and why must she call me Jerusha as if I were in her Latin class?" I could forgive poor old Grandpa his "little Jerusha," but she might come off her high horse enough to call me Jerry like the rest of the family.

"You look rested," she went on, scrutinizing me (for flaws, I thought). "There are strawberries for you to start off with. Chester brought them from his garden, especially for Freddy and you. I'll have your batter ready in a jiffy."

Aunt Edith brought me the strawberries and then the waffle batter, all yellow and foamy, along with a fresh supply of butter and syrup and beach-plum jelly. She didn't sit down with us, though. She went to the sink to start washing up. She was very efficient. In Grandma's time, my breakfasts were all hustle and bustle and laughter and fuss, with Grandma sitting down to chat with me, then leaping up becaue she'd forgotten the this or burned the that, and I loved it all, even the burnt toast, because I knew that for my Grandma I was so important that she couldn't remember other things. For Aunt Edith, though, I was just an item in her overall plan.

Freddy had slipped out of Grandpa's lap to take charge of the waffle iron. Grandpa didn't notice. He was probably thinking about his sermon. Freddy got so absorbed in measuring batter into the waffle iron to get just the right amount of gush, and I was so busy eating (I was starved), that we both forgot to remind Aunt Edith to remind Grandpa of his meeting. Aunt Edith remembered by herself at nine-thirty, and we all had to hustle to get Grandpa off. I found his hat and coat in the hall closet. Aunt Edith collected his notes from the study, and Freddy brushed the cat hairs off his trousers. While Freddy and I were helping him with gestures and advice on how to back the Electric out of the stable, Aunt Edith ran out with a piece of string. She tied it around Grandpa's finger to remind him to stop at Chester's garage on his way home, leave the Electric's battery to be charged, and have Chester or one of his mechanics put in the spare battery which was at the garage and had already been charged. Grandpa looked very handsome sitting up in the Electric in his wide-brimmed black hat, and we told him so. He smiled and waved, grasped the tiller, swung the Electric about, and rolled silently down the drive.

"Now, Jerusha," said Aunt Edith, "I've just got time to finish up in the kitchen, and you've just got time to write postcards to your mother and father, before Cousin Harriet and Mary come."

"Oh, no!" I wailed.

"What's the matter? I thought you'd like to see Mary. I thought you were friends."

I scowled at Aunt Edith. Then, because she raised her eyebrows in mock consternation (another of her schoolmarm tricks), I hung my head and scowled at my sneakers. It was true in a way that Mary and I were friends. We had played together, if you could call it play, ever since we were babies. This year, I guess because of all my other worries, I had completely forgotten that either Mary or her grandmother existed.

Aunt Edith went on: "When Cousin Harriet stopped by to say that she and Mary would come over to see you and Freddy this morning, after you'd rested from your journey, I couldn't very well tell her not to come, and I thought you'd be glad. I haven't seen poor Mary yet myself. I expect she's pretty lonely with no one her own age around, and anxious to see you again."

"I don't mind seeing Mary," I muttered, still scowling at my sneakers, "but I don't see why I have to see her just when Freddy and I had planned to go down to the cove and see Bron and dig clams for Grandpa's lunch."

"There'll be plenty of other times for digging clams and seeing Bron."

"No, there won't. The tide's just right now. There are plenty of other times for seeing Mary, though, and I don't care if I never see Cousin Harriet." After this show of defiance, I was afraid to look at Aunt Edith. I gave Freddy a quick sidelong glance which meant, "See, I told you she'd spoil everything," and went on scowling at my sneakers.

It seemed a long time before Aunt Edith spoke again.

"I'm sorry, Jerusha, that I've spoiled your plans for your first morning here, but I can't ask Cousin Harriet not to come now. There isn't time and, besides, she thinks she is doing us a favor. She would be offended."

"Tell her that I was called away on important business," I answered back, and was immediately uneasy about my sauciness.

Again Aunt Edith took a long time to reply. "No, Jerusha," she said at last, "I will not lie to Cousin Harriet or be rude to her. She is an older person, and a relative, and, in this case, meant no harm." There was a pause. "I might as well tell you now, Jerusha, that whether you like her or not, Cousin Harriet is necessary to us. If she did not contribute generously to your grandfather's church every year, the church couldn't afford a minister, and we couldn't afford to live here at The Haven. We'd have to sell it."

"Oh, no," cried Freddy.

I was shocked, too, at this revelation, but I wasn't going to give up gracefully.

"You mean you're going to *make* me stay to say 'How do you do' to Cousin Harriet and play with Mary?"

"If you want to put it that way, yes," said Aunt Edith, and I knew I was licked. "First, though," she went on, "you have your postcards to write. They are on the kitchen table." She turned to go in. "If Freddy wants to go to the cove for clams after he has said 'How do you do' to Cousin Harriet and Mary, he may. If Bron is there and awake enough to help him, the two should be able to get plenty of clams for lunch."

When I had finished my postcards, Freddy and I took them out to the RFD box by the front gate.

"I'm sorry," said Freddy, "but Auntie couldn't help it, and I thought she tried to be nice, only you wouldn't let her."

"I suppose so," I admitted. "Only she's so superior. She's like a schoolteacher, not an aunt." Echoing poor Grandpa, I went on, "Nothing is right anymore. I wanted so much to see Bron and dig clams with him and you, and, you know, I'd forgotten all about Mary. Aunt Edith would never believe that, but it's true."

"I believe it," said Freddy. "I forget her, too, as much as I can."

Poor Mary and the "It Girl"

WHAT FREDDY SAID made me think about Mary, or "poor Mary" as the grownups in our family always called her.

She was a year or so older than I, but small for her age and very quiet. She never said boo to her bossy old grandmother, who was bringing her up because her parents were dead. Every morning, before Mary could even come outdoors, her grandmother made her featherstitch a square of patchwork, or hemstitch a towel, or cross-stitch a doily, or chainstitch a handkerchief. Her grandmother's idea of a treat was to let her sew a dress for her doll. Her grandmother was always bragging about how well Mary sewed, and my own grandmother had often said that she wished I'd learn to sew half as well as poor Mary did, but she never made me, so I never did. Mary's grandmother chose all her clothes for her — brown or blue sailor dresses for everyday, and white ones for best — and all her books — sweet, old-fashioned stories about noble people doing noble deeds. Mary's grandmother chose her activities, too — jacks or Canfield for indoors, butterfly and flower collecting for outdoors. Mary was never allowed to play running games or climb trees or row or sail a boat. It wasn't until my own grandma got her dander up and told Cousin Harriet that it was downright dangerous to let a girl grow up not knowing how to swim, that the old lady let Mary take swimming lessons at the yacht club. She still didn't let Mary splash around unattended with Freddy and me at the cove. Mary never complained about the things she had to do or wasn't allowed to do, and she didn't seem to get much fun out of the things that were supposed to be fun for her. Her eyes were very big and brown and looked even bigger than they were because her face was so skinny (and all the rest of her, too). They were always darting around as if she was afraid, and I guess she was. Grownups always felt sorry for her, and sometimes I did, too, only I knew another Mary — Princess Mary — that they didn't know.

When Cousin Harriet went out for a whole afternoon and left Mary in my grandma's charge, "poor Mary" vanished and "Princess Mary" took her place.

At these times, we always had to play the games that Mary made up. They were all about princesses. There was "Princess rescued from the tower where Wicked Queen has imprisoned her," "Princess rescued from the dungeon where Wicked Queen, etc.," "Prince and Princess storm Wicked Queen out of her castle," and so on. Grandma had some old clothes in a chest that she let us dress up in. Since Mary was always the princess, she got the pretty dresses. As Prince or Knight, I got a red plush

portière for a cape and an old sword and belt that had belonged
to Great-Grandfather Haskell. As Wicked Queen, I always got
an ugly, old black cotton skirt and bodice. I argued that a
wicked queen should have as good clothes as a princess, but
Mary grabbed the pretty clothes first, and stamped her foot and
dared me to get them away from her; so, rather than tear the
dresses to bits, I let her keep them. Freddy, when Mary commandeered him to be an attendant knight or prince, got the
leftovers. Freddy hated Mary's games, but Mary teased, flattered, and bullied him into playing. Sometimes I let him have
the cape, belt, and sword. They tripped him up but made him
feel better.

I enjoyed climbing the stable roof to rescue Mary out of the
cupola, or letting myself down from the loft with a rope to
rescue Mary from Buster's old stall. Holding the hen house
(there were no hens) against the assaults of Mary and Freddy
was fun, except that I had to watch out not to hurt Mary or
break any more windows. After the action, Mary paraded
around in her princess costume spouting fancy, old-fashioned
words about how smart and beautiful she was, and what great
things she was going to do now that she was free. She ordered
Freddy to pull the wicked queen's (my) fingernails out and
then boil me in oil, or to cut out my eyes and serve them on a
silver platter for lunch. Freddy had nightmares about the nasty
things she told him to do to me. He was very young then, and
he always had a soft heart. My heart wasn't particularly soft,
but after a while Mary's games bored me. As Prince, I never
got to say anything but, "Most beauteous princess, how I adore
you," or stuff like that. Mary shut me up so she could rant on
and on. As Wicked Queen, I was only allowed to wallow at
Mary's feet, shrieking, "Mercy, mercy, most beauteous one," and

sometimes Mary spurned me with her heel harder than was necessary. I never got to make up games of my own, and I often threatened to strike, but Mary had me on the spot. She'd threaten to tell Grandma that I, not a northeast gale, had broken the windows in the hen house and loosened the shingles on the stable roof. She'd pull up her hair, which hung like a waterfall halfway down her back, to show me the cut I'd inflicted with my mace (I believe she scratched the scabs away as they formed to keep the thing open all one summer) and she said she would tell about that, too. Grandma, I knew, would never believe that I had done these things only because Mary made me, and Grandma hated liars.

As soon as Cousin Harriet got back from her meeting, or her bridge, or her shopping, Princess Mary vanished, and "poor Mary" reappeared.

Freddy and I shoved our cards into the RFD box and pushed up the little metal flag. As we turned back toward the house, Freddy nudged me.

"They're coming!"

He pointed toward the hen house and the field just to the east of it where Grandma had transplanted wild beach-plum bushes and cultivated them into big clumps which in September bore the fattest, most beautiful beach plums in the world. Sure enough, just above the bushes, swooped, floated, dipped, and hovered Cousin Harriet's summer hat. It was a memorable hat, swathed in veils, wreathed with flowers, and topped by a bunch of artificial cherries that clicked as Cousin Harriet walked.

"Why can't she come around by the road like other people?" Freddy demanded. "She's got no business in our field."

"She's looking over the beach plums," I said. "Grandma always let her have some to make jelly."

"She's got a nerve," said Freddy. "I'm going to tell Auntie."

We made for the house, but Cousin Harriet and her hat had speeded up, too. Before we could disappear into the shadow of the wisteria, she was bearing down on us. Like a ship's prow, her bosom sheared the air well in advance of the rest of her. Her long, old-fashioned skirt swirled about her feet like foam. The hat, for all its veils, fruits, and flowers, detracted not at all from Cousin Harriet's dignity. It became her, as pennants become a battleship. Even the clicking of the artificial cherries was formidable. Cousin Harriet hove to just in front of Freddy and me. She favored us each with a long stare, then held out to us, each in turn, her dry, freckled, old hand and said, "How-djado?" twice.

Freddy and I knew that the hand was not meant to be shaken and the question not meant to be answered. We each touched the hand with our fingers and muttered politely. Freddy bowed. I curtsied.

Cousin Harriet now stared over our heads at Aunt Edith, who had come out onto the porch to greet her.

"They've grown," announced Cousin Harriet, "but the beach plums look poorly. I suppose you've been too busy to fertilize them properly. It's a pity. I was counting on jelly to give away for Christmas."

"It is a pity, Cousin Harriet," replied Aunt Edith, "but the reason they look poorly is because of a late frost." She stopped speaking. "Is that . . . ?" I knew what Aunt Edith was staring at.

A flapper, a real flapper out of the movies, was coming toward us slowly and shakily because her high heels kept sinking into the grass.

Cousin Harriet glanced over her shoulder. "Hurry up, Mary.

I told you not to wear those silly shoes to walk through the field. You might sprain your ankle."

"Oh, leave me alone. I have to break them in, don't I?"

Cousin Harriet took no notice of this. She swept onto our porch as if she owned it and settled herself in the best chair. Mary stopped at the edge of the drive. She fluffed up her bob. She patted the kerchief (red to match her lips) which was knotted around her throat and pinned to her blouse at one shoulder. She wiggled her hip so her white butterfly skirt swung, and as she preened herself, a collection of bracelets such as Cleopatra might have envied clanked up and down her forearms.

"Hi, Cousin Edith." She tossed a smile at Aunt Edith and clinked and clanked across the driveway right up to Freddy.

"How's my old boy friend?" Mary gave Freddy a playful poke in the ribs.

Freddy stared at her. "You wear lipstick," he said.

"Like it?" Mary cocked her head and smiled.

"I hate it." Freddy's face flushed. "I'm not your boy friend. I wouldn't be your boy friend for a million dollars." He turned and ran away down the drive.

"He's a scream," said Mary. "Give him a few more years and I bet he'll change his mind." She turned her attention to me. Those big, brown eyes that used to be so frightened gave me the once-over as coolly as old Sunbeam had at breakfast. I took it from Sunbeam, but I resented it from Mary.

"See enough?" I asked.

"You still look young, all right, even for your age." Mary yawned and went on, as if to make the best of a dreary situation, "Let's get away from The Hag at least and go up to your room or somewhere where we can talk."

"The Hag?" I was completely at sea.

"My grandmother." Mary laughed. "That's what I call her. Come on upstairs. I can tell you a thing or two."

Without a by-your-leave or an excuse-me, Mary marched, clanking, right between Aunt Edith and her grandmother, into the house, up the stairs, and into my room. I followed.

She marched straight through my room to the open window, raised the screen, and leaned out. She stayed half out the window for a long time. When she finally came back in, she was holding a swath of wisteria leaves which she waved thoughtfully in front of her.

"What do you think you're doing?" I asked.

"Checking," replied Mary. "I have to know what The Hag is saying about me, how much she knows about what I'm doing, and what her line is going to be when she talks to my guardian, that sort of stuff. Then I can tell *my* side first." Mary smiled to herself. "I've really scared the pants off The Old Hag. She hasn't tried any funny business for a long time, but I keep tabs." Dismissing "The Hag" with a toss of her head, Mary suddenly stuck the wisteria swath in the corner of her mouth. Setting her feet apart, she began to vibrate all over, and clasping both hands on one hip, she batted her eyes at me. Through her mouthful of wisteria, she flashed a provocative grin.

She removed the wisteria and asked, "What movie star was I being?"

"Clara Bow," I said. "The 'It Girl.' Only you ought to have red hair."

Mary accepted my knowledgeableness as a compliment. "I *am* a good actress. I'm rinsing my hair with henna once a week. Mrs. Munson gets it for me, and she says if the henna doesn't work, she knows a place in New York where I can get it dyed.

Mrs. Munson says I ought to be a movie star. She says I have talent."

Mary's complacency was beginning to annoy me. "I'd like to hear what your grandmother says when you walk in with red hair."

"It doesn't matter what she says," replied Mary. "Everything is changed. I might as well tell you about it. I haven't anything else to do until twelve. Then Mrs. Munson is taking me over to the yacht club for lunch." Mary surveyed the furniture of my room. "You ought to have a chess lounge," she said, "for lounging. Oh well, I'll just have to stretch out on the bed." She kicked her off her shoes and shoved back my sunshine-and-shadow quilt. "I can't stand to look at those patchwork things." She reeled back in horror as if she were seeing a corpse. "They remind me of all the awful stuff The Hag used to make me sew. Take it away!"

I grabbed the quilt, folded it, and laid it on my bureau. "I don't let people lie on it anyway," I said. "My grandmother made it for me."

Mary was settling herself on my bed. "Your grandmother wasn't like mine, so you don't know how I feel about these things. I'm sorry she died — I mean *your* grandmother. I don't think I'll exactly cry my eyes out when The Hag kicks the bucket. Now" — Mary wriggled her head and shoulders into a comfortable position against my pillow — "I guess I'd better start at the beginning, when we moved back to New York at the end of last summer. The Hag got another telephone put in upstairs because of her rheumatism, and I got the bright idea of listening in on the calls. Up till then" — Mary clicked her tongue and rolled her eyes — "I was a real Dumb Dora. The things I didn't know would fill a book. I didn't even know that

I was rich, or that besides The Hag, I had a guardian, and that he didn't approve of the way The Hag was bringing me up, only he was afraid of her. Whew!" Mary rolled her eyes some more. "I learned about what the cook does nights and about Ella's boy friends (she's the second maid), but I haven't time to tell all that now."

I sat down on the straight chair by the window. Mary went on.

"Uncle Edward — that's what I call this guardian, though he's not really my uncle — kept telling The Hag how he thought it was high time I had clothes like other girls, and walked back and forth to school with the girls, instead of being driven, and did things with them afternoons, like shopping or going to movies or just fooling around, and went to parties, and met some boys. The Hag always told him that when I was eighteen and ready to come out, then it would be time enough for shopping and movies and parties and boys. She said I never complained about my clothes, or my sewing, or my practicing. She was right. I was just too dumb. She said I never asked to go around with other girls. She was right there, too. I didn't care about girls then, and I still don't, but, boy! Was I dumb!"

"After I'd done my sewing and my practicing, I used to make up stories and act them out by myself or with Ella and the cook, only they giggled too much. I'm good at making up stories. I still do it for fun sometimes, but mostly to get things I want. The stories I make up now aren't the old babyish kind I made up out of what I'd read in books and acted out with you and Freddy or Ella and the cook. Not by a long shot!"

Mary dug herself deeper into my pillows and let out a long, self-satisfied sigh. "All the arguing between Uncle Edward and

The Hag gave me my second bright idea. I wrote a letter to Uncle Edward. I started off saying how I didn't know him very well, and I was scared he'd think I was fresh, but that he'd seemed awfully sweet the few times I'd met him, and after all he was my guardian, and I was desperate. Then I told him how miserable I was because The Hag wouldn't let me do any of the things I wanted to, which were, of course, all the things I'd heard old Uncle tell The Hag over the telephone that she should let me do. It must have been a pretty good letter, because WOW!"

Mary sprang to her feet and jumped up and down on my bed until she collapsed, giggling, in the mess she had made of my bedclothes. "What a stink!" She caught her breath and went on. "Old Uncle got up his courage and accused The Hag of cruelty to me. The Hag told him she'd thank him to stick to managing my money so I wouldn't grow up to be a pauper, and to keep his nose out of my other affairs, which he was too stupid to understand, and she wondered if he was competent to manage my money even, and if she maybe shouldn't have him investigated and sued for negligence. She was tough, but old Uncle stood his ground pretty well. He said he'd report The Hag to the S.P.C.C., and finally he got her to agree to send me to a boarding school."

Mary stirred up my bedclothes some more and turned reflective. "I should never have let them send me to that boarding school, but I didn't know any better. I thought it was great just to go out with Ella to the stores and buy some school uniforms, and boots and things for winter, and put them on and go away. I had a lot to learn, and I guess I learned faster at that boarding school than I would have almost anywhere else. My time wasn't entirely wasted, but UGH!" Mary shuddered.

"The school was somewhere up here in Massachusetts, in a little one-horse town. You'd never have heard of it. It was November when I got there, and I nearly froze because it was a wholesome school, and they never let the heat go above sixty-five. Of course, they really kept the place cold to save money, but old Fish-Face, she was the headmistress, had a spiel about how her girls dressed sensibly, got plenty of exercise, both mental and physical, and grew up to have some blah, blah, blah in Latin. The Hag loved that spiel. She used to quote it at her bridge club.

"We had classes all morning, except when they sent us out to run around the playing field so we wouldn't freeze to our chairs. In the afternoon, we raced around waving hockey sticks, only we weren't allowed to hit each other, which would have made some sense, but just an old ball. After supper, we studied some more. On Saturdays, we were all herded to a dirty, cold cabin on a hill where we had to cook hot dogs and play silly games. Sundays we went to church and studied some more, and Fish-Face read to us out of uplifting books. I don't know how I stood it as long as I did."

Mary paused, shaking her head in wonder at her own endurance. "There were two kinds of girls at that school," she went on, "wholesome ones that fitted, and ones that weren't wholesome and didn't. Neither kind liked me much, and vice versa. As soon as I'd tried studying and exercising and being wholesome long enough to know I definitely didn't go for *that,* I started tagging after the unwholesome girls. They picked on me at first, and I'll always hate them for it. I hate them even more than the wholesome ones, actually. They were just sort of limited and immature. Like you, Jerry."

"Thanks," I said.

"Don't get sore," replied Mary. "You know what I mean, and anyway it's not important. School wasn't so bad after I got in with the unwholesome crowd. They gave me tips about how to dress and use make-up. Believe it or not, I didn't even own a compact when I went to school. They lent me movie magazines and *True Story* and some even better ones that, of course, we weren't allowed to have. Sometimes, at night, a few of them would get together in someone's room with candy or maybe cigarettes, only they were awfully dangerous because of the smell, and they'd tell dirty jokes or talk about the boys they knew and kissing and sex, or how they hated their parents or the teachers or the wholesome girls. At first, I just sat and listened, and they didn't pay any attention to me — which was okay, because at first I didn't get the jokes or understand what they were talking about. I caught on pretty fast, though. When I told them how much I hated The Hag, they perked up and began to pay some attention to me. I told how I'd fooled her with the letter, and I made up some things I'd done with boys that I hadn't really, and those girls — they were pretty dumb, too — listened to me and had some respect for me. It was exciting — huddled in the dark, knowing that if a teacher or student government officer caught us we'd get it." Mary shuddered luxuriously.

"Later, in the spring, after I'd been to a few concerts and dances with a boys' school that was at the other end of this little one-horse place, I had some real boy friends. Sometimes, when some of us girls got permission to go downtown, we'd arrange to meet the boys. We'd go behind Merrill's Market where they kept the old crates, and hide, and fool around, and neck." Mary favored me with a condescending smile. "I expect you're shocked to hear that I neck. Well, all I can say is that I got off to a slow start, but I work fast once I get going."

Mary jumped off the bed and strutted around the room, snapping her fingers and rolling her eyes and hips. "I do this to shock The Hag when she has guests. I learned it from watching Clara Bow. Aren't I good?" Mary didn't wait for me to answer. "Sometimes I do this." She broke into a Charleston which set the furniture rattling. "Drives The Old Hag crazy." And Mary laughed and threw herself back onto my bed.

"It was behind Merrill's Market that I met Ken. He didn't go to the boys' school. He was a senior in the high school, and he drove Merrill's delivery truck after school to make money. He was a lot more mature than those prep-school boys, and he was crazy about me." Mary heaved a sigh. "At night, after work, sometimes, he'd drive the delivery truck right up to the back of the school, as if he was delivering something, and I'd get in the back with him, and OH BOY!" Mary gave a couple of ecstatic writhes. "Only I almost got caught. I had to lie like anything. The head of the student government didn't really believe me, though she couldn't prove I was lying. But she had it in for me anyway. She took away all my permissions and got my roommate to spy on me. I'd had all I could take of that school. I'd learned all they could teach me there, so what was the point of going on with those stupid games and classes and putting up with all those girls I couldn't stand?" Mary shrugged. "I decided to run away. I planned it carefully. I managed to sneak out long enough to see Ken. I told him my plan. He'd do anything for me. He was absolutely nuts about me. I got back to school without getting caught. The next night he drove the delivery truck up to the back door at nine o'clock just when I was getting out of late study hall. I'd fixed my bed to look as if I was asleep in it, and I'd stashed a suitcase in the lilac bush by the kitchen door. I grabbed the suitcase and popped into the back of the delivery truck. We were off in a jiffy, and Ken drove me all the way in to South Station in Boston. When he was putting me on the train for New York, he said if I ever needed help again to call on him. He said he was my knight. Wasn't that cute? Poor Ken, I guess I've sort of outgrown him since, but he's still crazy about me." Mary hugged herself and smiled up at the ceiling, too entranced by her own fatal charm to go on.

"So what happened?" I prodded her.

She came to. "Early the next morning before anyone at the dear old school even knew I'd skipped, I was at Uncle Edward's apartment. Pretty neat, wasn't it?"

I had to admit it was.

"At school," continued Mary, "they thought I was dumb because I didn't study and failed the tests, but I'm not dumb, not at things I'm interested in. All the way down on the train, I planned what I'd say to Uncle Edward. He opened the door to the apartment himself, in his bathrobe, with his eyes half shut. I cried a little — not enough to scare him — just to give him time to wake up and see how pathetic I was and feel sorry for me. When he finally seemed to be clicking, I told the story I'd planned. I was at a terrible disadvantage at school in my studies, and socially too because of the cruel way The Hag had brought me up. All year, up to now, I told him, I'd tried to overcome my disadvantages and stick it out because I knew he wanted me to. I'd cried myself to sleep every night, and I'd had dizzy spells in classes which kept me from learning, and all the running and jumping around they made me do gave me a pain over my heart, only I never mentioned these things before so as not to worry him. The pain in the heart was terrible." Mary whacked herself on the chest, slumped over, and writhed. When she sat up, she actually had tears on her cheeks. " 'I couldn't stand it any longer, Uncle Edward,' " she cried, holding out her arms to me. " 'I came to you because you are the only one who understands me. Grandmother doesn't and never will. Let me stay with you here and be your daughter.' " Mary's voice subsided on a high, anguished note. She went back to her regular voice. "Whew, I guess I carried myself away that time. I've sure got a lot of temperament." She jumped off the bed, ran to my dresser, and began making faces at herself in the mirror. I had to prod her to go on again. She tore herself away from her reflection and sat on the edge of my bed.

"If Fish-Face hadn't got on the phone about then, I think I'd have brought old Uncle around. He'd been acting kind of stiff and funny, but I'd have got through to him. At least I think I would. Fish-Face must have given him an earful. Uncle didn't have an extension on his phone, so I had no way of knowing what Fish-Face said. She talked a long time, and I guess she knew a lot. Some of my dear friends must have squealed on me. If I ever get a chance to play a mean trick on any of them, I'll take it." Mary narrowed her eyes, then laughed. "Oh well, it doesn't matter. To make a long story short, he imprisoned me in his apartment all day, with his fright of a housekeeper watching me like a vulture, while he had more chats with Fish-Face and went to see The Hag and a lawyer. In the evening, he sat me down in the most uncomfortable chair in his study and said he would make a bargain with me, and if I kept my part, he'd keep his. He said he couldn't possibly have me living with him or running to him every time I was in trouble. He said he wasn't qualified to look after wayward girls. Somehow I thought he didn't sound friendly. I broke in and said that if he thought I was going back to that school, he was crazy. He laughed then, a sort of funny laugh. He said I needn't worry. He said that school wouldn't take me back, even if he gave them all my common stock as a bribe. He said there were only two places that would take me — one was The Hag, the other was a special school for stubborn girls. He said he hoped I'd choose to go back to The Hag, because he was sure I wouldn't like the special school, and it wouldn't be easy to run away from. He said The Hag, for all her faults, loved me in her peculiar way, and she had agreed to let me do as I pleased within certain limits, which he and The Hag and the lawyer had agreed on together. I could see that Fish-Face had really poisoned his mind against me. I said it seemed to me that I should have some say in what I could and couldn't do if I went back to The Hag. He said he agreed with me, and he'd had all the regulations that he and The Hag and the lawyer had made up typed on a piece of paper so I could read them. He gave me the list and told me to read it, and if I found any of the regulations unreasonable, he'd be glad to discuss them with me.

"Well, I read the regulations, and they weren't too bad, so I agreed to them, and I went back to The Hag. I get an allowance, and I buy my own clothes, and I didn't have to go to school all the rest of the spring term. The lawyer is looking into schools for me for next fall." Mary laughed. "He's having a tough time finding one that's brave enough to take me. In New York, before we came up here, all I had to do was tell Ella where I was going when I went out, and be in time for meals. I saw at least two movies every day. That was great. The rules about going out nights are too strict, but I didn't fuss about them because, in New York, I can always get out by the fire escape, and here all I have to do is tell The Hag I'm going somewhere with Mrs. Munson, so I'm all right."

"You're not keeping your side of the bargain, though," I said.

Mary's eyes flicked over me. "You're a scream," she said. Neither her voice nor her expression betrayed a trace of mirth. She dug around in her bracelets and found a watch.

"Eleven-thirty." She yawned. She sauntered over to my mirror again and became absorbed in her face. "I don't suppose you have a lipstick?" she asked.

"No."

"I didn't think you would, but it doesn't matter because Mrs. Munson will lend me hers." Mary sauntered back to the bed. "Watch this!" She sat herself down, twisted her shoulders one way and her neck the other, hiked her skirt above her knees, crossed them, and leered at me. "Mrs. Munson and I are just like that." Mary held up two fingers and winked.

"That's great, Clara," I said, "but who's Mrs. Munson?"

"Oh, I forgot you don't know her. The Munsons rent The Hag's other cottage."

"How nice for them."

Sarcasm was wasted on Mary. "It is nice," she said. "Mrs. Munson has done a lot for me because she recognizes my talent."

I pointedly didn't ask what, beyond recommending hair-dyeing establishments and lending lipsticks, Mrs. Munson had done for Mary. I even yawned to indicate that Mary bored me, but Mary was impervious to outside influences.

"I might as well tell you about the Munsons. There's nothing else for me to do until twelve." She arranged my pillows in a new way, draped herself over them, and proceeded to tell me about the Munsons.

They were peppy and cute — not like the drippy schoolteachers The Hag usually rented her other cottage to. Mr. Munson was terribly busy and away from home a lot because he was floating his own new cosmetic company, called Dagmar — wasn't that the cutest name? — because Dagmar was Mrs. Munson's first name. Mrs. Munson was doing her darndest to help Mr. Munson make a go of Dagmar. Dagmar was the kind of cosmetic company that used saleswomen to call on people in their homes, show them the Dagmar line, and take their orders. Dagmar saleswomen always tried to sell the type of cosmetic that was right for the individual buyer. It was a very personal company, and it cared. Mrs. Munson went out two or three times a week to call on people and introduce them to the Dagmar line by giving them free samples. She was very frank and sincere. She believed in Dagmar, and she said quite openly that she had come to Sewell to make contacts with rich summer people who would use Dagmar products and tell their friends about them. Mrs. Munson had called on The Hag the very day that Mary and The Hag arrived at their cottage. She brought a bunch of flowers, her cosmetic kit, and samples. While Mrs. Munson was giving out samples to The Hag, and The Hag was gloating over getting so much for nothing, Mary walked in in her new red bathing suit which she wore around a lot because it shocked The Hag. The minute Mrs. Munson saw Mary, she knew that she was in the presence of Talent.

"It was just from the way I walked and the way I held my head that she knew." Mary rearranged my pillows and redraped herself. "Mrs. Munson asked The Hag if she might make me up to show how good Dagmar products were. She told The Hag that with Dagmar rouges and eye make-ups she could highlight my best features, and brighten my complexion, and that when she got through, I would look as if I had no make-up on at all, only I'd be even more beautiful than usual. The Hag was so happy about the free samples that she didn't object, and, you know, when Mrs. Munson finished me, I did look perfectly natural and perfectly beautiful. I bought a whole bunch of the stuff. The Hag, of course, was too stingy to buy anything but a box of face powder. While I was walking out with Mrs. Munson, across the yard to her cottage, she told me I had a real actress's face, and she'd be glad to show me more make-up techniques. She said just to come over any afternoon when I saw her banana wagon with 'Dagmar' written on it in the garage.

"Believe you me, I didn't let a chance like that go by. I was over the next day. Mrs. Munson showed me all sorts of things you can do with make-up. Mrs. Munson and I have got to be real pals. I never thought I could be pals the way we are with anyone, least of all a grown-up woman, but I guess I never knew any grown-up women except for The Hag and her awful friends, and schoolteachers. Naturally, I hated them. I told Mrs. Munson all about myself. She said that she had been brought up strictly herself and knew what I was going through. I told her how dull it was for me here all summer. I told her I would have liked to fool around more at the yacht club, but I didn't know any of the kids there, and I had to either walk down by myself, or wait until The Hag had ordered a car and driver, which she only did when it suited her, with no consideration of me at all. I was hardly seeing any movies either, just the one on Saturday at the Grange Hall, and that was usually so old I'd already seen it. Besides, The Hag always had me driven down and picked up afterward. It wasn't much fun. Mrs. Munson said she knew I couldn't develop my talent if I wasn't free and happy and never saw any movies, and she wanted to help me. She said that if only she and Mr. Munson belonged to the yacht club she could drive me there and chaperone me while she made contacts for Dagmar. This would help us both. I helped persuade The Hag to propose Mr. Munson and her for membership in the club. The Hag didn't need much persuading. All she had to do was tell the governors of the yacht club to make the Munsons members and she had me off her hands for practically the whole summer. She was getting something for nothing. Of course, everyone around here does whatever The Hag asks them to because they hope to get money out of her later. They don't usually get much, but you can't blame them for trying."

Mary paused a moment. "I suppose if The Hag weren't rich, she wouldn't dare be so bossy, but what do I care about her? For me now everything is hunky-dory. Every day I can get driven to the yacht club, and if I get tired of fooling around there, Mrs. Munson will almost always drop me off at a movie when she goes out to make her Dagmar calls and pick me up on her way back. She says she'd like to take me with her and use me as a model for Dagmar demonstrations, but she's afraid The Hag might not approve, so she just leaves me at the movies. She's really a swell person. At the yacht club, everyone likes her — grownups and kids both. There's never a dull moment when she's around, and she's always giving out samples and making contacts. Even Bron comes in off his boat when she's there, and sits and talks to her, and when he's there, oh boy, do I ever stick around." Mary hugged herself and rolled her eyes. "Because, I might as well tell you, he's my latest hearthrob."

"What's Bron doing down there?" I'd forgotten that I was bored.

"Waiting to take people on boat rides and fishing trips. That's where he picks them up and leaves them, or right next door at the town wharf. I've been out with him once already with a bunch of the kids. Mrs. Munson arranged it, and The Hag paid for it. It was meant to help me get to know the kids, but, golly, once I'd got an eyeful of Bron, I didn't care if the other kids were there or not." An ecstatic shudder convulsed Mary. When she'd got over it, she went on. "It's funny I never noticed him before this year, and now I can't look at him without going all goose pimples. Poor Ken. He was a nice kid, and I'll go on writing him, but I really have outgrown him."

"What makes you think Bron would notice you?"

"Nothing, right now, but I'm working on him." Mary gave another of her Clara Bow leers.

"It won't get you anywhere. Bron can't stand flappers or movie actresses or — or liars." I was immediately ashamed of myself for being so nasty, but I needn't have been. I hadn't hurt Mary's feelings a bit.

"Honestly, Jerry, you take the cake. If you have any idea that Bron ever thinks of *you* as anything but a wholesome little girl with freckles, forget it, and I'm not the only one who's after him. All the cute older girls at the club are crazy about him too, and, of course, your Aunt Edith has been sweet on him for years, only she's so stuck-up and prissy she can't act natural and show it. She's a real lemon. She doesn't even make the most of her looks. Mrs. Munson could show her a thing or two."

"My Aunt Edith wouldn't touch Mrs. Munson or any of her face powder or any of that fast yacht club crowd with a ten-foot pole," I shouted, and stopped, astonished at what I had said.

"Okay, Jerry. Okay. Keep your pants on. You really are too wholesome to be true. Just try to get it through your head that I have as good a right as anyone to Bron, and as good a chance of getting him too, and I'm telling you now, as a friend, that you'd better not try anything with him because you don't know how, and besides you just haven't any sex appeal."

I wanted to hit Mary or at least shrivel her with my mordant wit. All I could think of to say was, "Oh yeah, well you're not as smart as you think you are. So there!"

Unperturbed, Mary rose, smoothed her skirt, fluffed her bob, and proceeded to the door. There she turned, placed both hands on her left hip, and began to jiggle again all over. "Sorry," she said, out of the side of her mouth. "No offense meant, but take it from me, honey, it's the truth that hurts." She winked, opened the door, flapped a hand at me, and jiggled and clanked away.

Even while I burned with fury at Mary, I worried. I was sure I despised her, yet she made me feel that I and all my family were somehow contemptible, and that my most cherished beliefs were childish and absurd. Most disturbing of all, she made me doubt Bron. Could Bron, our Bron, really have become a hanger-around of the yacht club, the pal of cheap summer people, the boy friend of rich flappers? Impossible! He was too proud. Yet he must hang around the yacht club, or Mary wouldn't be seeing him there, and he certainly wasn't hanging around us at The Haven. He hadn't come to see Freddy and me last night, or at breakfast either, and poor Grandpa had complained that Bron never came to see him anymore and seemed to feel uncomfortable at The Haven. Mary was gone, but her poison lingered on, and she'd left a nasty, dirty, perfumy smell in my room too. I raised the screen and stuck my head out for some gulps of clean, fresh air. Mary was still clanking down below on the porch under the wisteria.

"So long," I heard her say.

"Will you be home by dinner time?" demanded Cousin Harriet.

"Duntesk," replied Mary, and clanked away.

"When you remember, Edith, the care I have lavished on that girl, you must surely sympathize with me." Cousin Harriet's voice rose up, harsh and loud. " 'So long,' 'Don't ask,' indeed! What sort of talk is that, and to me, her grandmother, who has sacrificed so much for her?"

"I know it is hard for you, Cousin Harriet, and I believe that manners are important." Aunt Edith was using her best consultation-with-the-parent voice. "Since the war, rules of behavior have so relaxed and become so confused that it is hard to judge anyone nowadays by manners alone. Girls Mary's age are especially apt to make a bad impression, without really meaning to. They don't know if they are women or children. They haven't any idea how to behave. Even after the best bringing-up, many of them are rude and rebellious. I have had them in class, and I find them very trying. I'm glad to say, though, that most of them outgrow this awkward stage and become quite pleasant and sensible."

Immediately Cousin Harriet gave voice again.

"I dare say you have a point, Edith, but I can't accept a comparison of my granddaughter with the girls you teach in the public high school. My granddaughter's birth and fortune alone set her above ordinary girls. She has a superior mind, and, until Edward Norton interfered, I saw to it that she had a superior education. No, the blame for the shocking change in Mary lies squarely with Edward Norton, and now he has the gall to go off to Europe for the summer and leave me all alone with her. That lawyer is no help at all. I believe Edward pays him an extra salary just for disagreeing with me and making my life difficult."

Cousin Harriet's sigh was almost as loud as her voice. "I am not a young woman. If Mrs. Munson hadn't come along to take some of the burden off my shoulders, I should be having a nervous breakdown this very minute." Aunt Edith clucked. "I don't usually have anything to do with my tenants socially," Cousin Harriet continued, "but, from the first, I felt the Munsons were a cut above the ordinary. He is in cosmetics, and she helps him. I have some stock in cosmetics myself. Of course, the Munsons adore my cottage and the view over the marshes right out to the open sea, and the feeling they get up here on the hill of being out of the rush and bustle of business.

"Mrs. Munson is very sensitive. The very first time she came to call, she sensed that I was at my wits' end over Mary. She is appreciative, too. I don't know how many times she — and her husband, too — has thanked me for letting them rent my garage as well as the one that goes with their cottage. Orders for the cosmetics were coming in so fast that they couldn't keep enough stock on hand to fill them. They needed storage space nearer than the main warehouse in Boston. I don't use the garage myself, and I was happy to oblige them. I've quite enjoyed dropping over to see Mrs. Munson of an evening when Mr. Munson was working late, and I could get away without Mary. Mary spends hours locked in her room talking to herself. It makes me nervous. As I said, Mrs. Munson is a sensitive person, and it was she who first mentioned that I seemed nervous about Mary. I would never have mentioned it myself. You know I am not one to talk about myself and my troubles. First and last, Mrs. Munson and I have had a great many talks about Mary. Mrs. Munson believes that now the harm to Mary has been done (thanks to Edward Norton), it is wisest to give her a long rein and keep an eye on her. She suggested that Mary would enjoy meeting the young people at the yacht club, and she said that, if only she were a member of the club, she herself would be willing to take Mary there several times a week and act as her chaperone. It would give her a chance to make more contacts and sell more cosmetics. As you know, Edith, I have never mixed with the fast crowd there myself. Many of them have risen quite recently from the lower classes. However, I consider Mrs. Munson to be intelligent and, for a woman who works, well-bred. I cannot see that any harm can come to Mary under Mrs. Munson's chaperonage. I told the commodore of the yacht club to see that the Munsons were elected members, and of course he did. It's a great relief to me to have Mary taken care of. I haven't noticed any improvement in her manners, but Mrs. Munson says we must be patient. Rome wasn't built in a day.

"Well, well," Cousin Harriet went on after a pause, "I expect Mrs. Bates has finished cleaning up the cottage and has my lunch ready. I really quite enjoy roughing it here with Mrs. Bates to help out. Of course, she and I are both sewing away for the bazaar. I'm only playing bridge once a week until I finish the aprons I promised. I've enjoyed talking with you, Edith. I may bring the Munsons to call one day. They are good Congregationalists, and have expressed a wish to meet Wilfred, and Mrs. Munson seems to have taken quite a fancy to this queer old house. She'd like to see the inside." Chairs scraped on the floor as the two ladies got up. "You will enjoy the Munsons, Edith, and I will ask them to bring you some of their samples."

"Please don't bother, Cousin Harriet. I never use make-up."

"Never mind that. They are free." The porch door opened and shut. Cousin Harriet swept off.

Aunt Edith sighed and walked indoors.

Bron

THE SILENCE after Cousin Harriet was very sweet. I went on leaning out my window, breathing in the sunlight and the familiar Sewell fragrances which I loved: freshness of flowers, arborvitae, and a salty moistness from the sea. Gradually peace of mind returned to me. I even felt a faint (very faint) sympathy for Mary. How could anyone be decent with a grandmother like hers?

"Auntie, Auntie, come look! We've got scads of clams!" It was Freddy's voice.

Freddy and Bron were coming up the drive together. Bron was carrying the clam hooks and basket. His hands and hip boots were all muddy, but his face was clean and tanned and smiling, and his hair shone like gold in the sunlight. He threw back his head and laughed.

"Hey, Edy, come see!" He held out the clam basket. "How's that for Freddy's first morning's work?"

Aunt Edith was walking down the drive to meet them. She looked into the clam basket.

"Good for you, Freddy," she cried. "You've got so many we can all have some for lunch." She patted Freddy's head and laughed. She looked at Bron. "It's been a long time since we've seen you. I was beginning to think you were avoiding us." She didn't sound happy anymore. She sounded like a schoolteacher.

Bron smiled down at her. "Don't be silly, Edy. Of course I'm not avoiding you. The season's started. *Irene* and I are busy. May I stay for lunch?"

"Don't *you* be silly. Of course you can," said Aunt Edith. The three of them came on up the driveway.

"Where's Jerry?" asked Bron. "I hear she had to stay home and do her duty by Mary."

I wanted to shout, "Here I am," and race down to hug him, but suddenly I felt shaky and shy. He and the others passed on toward the back of the shed where they would hose off the clams. I ran to my mirror and examined my face. I did look awfully wholesome. Would Dagmar cosmetics bring out some hidden allure in those round blue eyes, or make my nose less pug, or cover my freckles with the creamy luster of magnolia petals? I doubted it. I brushed my hair. Before I went downstairs I stopped in the bathroom to wash my face and hands and brush my teeth. My heart was thumping, and I was actually trembling as I rounded the back of the shed and presented myself to Bron.

He jumped up from beside the washtub where he was squatting and scrubbing clams. He smothered me in a bear hug, then swung me around so my feet flew up in the air.

"At last," he cried, and held me off at arm's length, as Grandpa had, to get a good look at me. "You've grown," he said, "but you're still the same, still my dear, old Jerry. It's great to have you back."

"It's great to be back," I said, full of happiness.

"We kept hoping you would come down and help us. Mary must have talked your ear off."

"She did," I said, "and I wanted to get away, but she was my guest, and I had to be polite."

Bron laughed. "You're a real lady, Jerry, and you have a look of your grandmother about you that would make me love you even if I didn't love you anyway."

"Oh, Bron," I cried. I thought I might burst with happiness.

"When you didn't come to help with the clams, I was afraid that maybe over the winter you'd turned into a silly little flapper like your friend Mary. Whew!" He gave an exaggerated sigh of relief and grinned at me. "Come on, get to work and help us scrub."

While we were scrubbing away, the Electric bearing Grandpa home to lunch rolled up the drive and into the stable. Bron went to welcome Grandpa home. Freddy and I finished scrubbing the clams and carried them into the kitchen for Aunt Edith to steam.

We had such a merry lunch. Grandpa was happy to see Bron, and he loved the steamed clams. He talked about his meeting, and how well the ladies were working together on the bazaar, bean supper, fireworks display, and dance, which, as always, would be held at the church on July 4th. Grandpa described with gusto what kind of rockets would soar and burst above the steeple, the varieties of pinwheel that would spit gobbets of colored fire, and the enormous American flag that, to climax the show, would sizzle red, white, and blue while the high school band played "The Star-Spangled Banner." The rest of us *ooh*ed and *aah*ed, and Freddy got so excited that I guess he thought he could go up like a rocket. Anyway he fell out of his chair. No one scolded him. We all laughed.

Later Bron teased Aunt Edith about not knowing enough geometry to teach it at Sewell High School, which she was going to have to do in the autumn, along with Latin and American history, because she had given up what Bron called her "plushy job" in Boston so she could stay at The Haven and look after Grandpa. He said such funny things, and Aunt Edith (I could hardly believe it) was just as funny answering him back. I thought she made snappier comebacks even than Bebe Daniels in the movies. She did an imitation of Cousin Harriet that had us all (even Grandpa) in stitches, and then I did an imitation of Mary imitating Clara Bow that put everyone in stitches again. Bron laughed more than anyone. For me, at any rate, it was his being there and noticing me that made me feel so easy and happy and able to say clever things without worrying whether other people would think they were clever. I guess he made us all feel good. I had never seen Aunt Edith act so young and undignified. Grandpa talked about Grandma without even sighing, but as if she were out of the room for a minute and would be right back to join the fun. When we had sent Grandpa off for his nap, Bron said why didn't we all go for a sail in the catboat.

"I've painted and caulked her," he said to me, "and put in

a new centerboard (the old one was rusted out), but I've been too busy to try her out. The tide's coming in, and there'll be a good breeze in the bay."

Freddy and I said we were all set to go.

Bron put his arm around Aunt Edith's waist, as she stood at the sink. "How about it, Edy? I know you're no great athlete like our Jerry here, but with us enthusiasts to urge you on, I bet you could learn to sail and enjoy it. After all, you're going to be a native Sewellian again. You can't go on acting like a landlubber."

Aunt Edith patted Bron's hand at her waist, turned to smile at us all, but shook her head. "You're nice to ask me, Bron, but I guess I just am a landlubber and too old to change." She moved away from Bron to dry her hands at the roller towel on the shed door. "I'd love to walk down to the cove with the rest of you and watch you set off. I'm not such a land-lubber that I don't enjoy watching experts like you and Jerry handle a boat, but after I've watched you sail away, I'll go on to the library and get some geometry books."

She turned to look straight at Bron. "You're right about my not knowing much, and maybe you can help me. Maybe, later, we can work together on it evenings the way we used to?" She smiled and waited for Bron to answer her. I couldn't help noticing again how beautiful she was, especially now when she wasn't being brusque but sort of hopeful and hum-ble and anxious to please. No amount of Dagmar cosmetics would ever make me, or anyone else for that matter, as beau-tiful as she was.

For a minute I was afraid that Bron would change his mind about sailing and offer to go to the library with Aunt Edith. He didn't. He muttered something vague about not knowing much geometry himself, stared at the floor for a minute, then shrugged, and turned to Freddy and me.

"Get the sail, and your sweaters and your bathing suits too, if you like. You can change on *Irene* and have a swim when we get back. Step lively."

At the cove the tide was high and a breeze ruffled the water into lively wavelets. Water, sky, and our newly painted catboat were all bright and brisk and shiny. Only *Irene,* instead of her usual buttercup yellow, was painted a dismal black.

"I don't like it," said Freddy. "She looks like a pirate ship."

Bron sighed. "I'm sorry, Freddy. You see, most women look their best in black, and I thought *Irene* would too. I realize now that I was wrong. *Irene* is the sort of girl who should only wear pastels. I bet you'll like her inside though. She's prettier and more comfortable than ever. I'll show you 'round later."

Bron rowed us out to the catboat in our skiff, and we all climbed aboard. "From now on," said Bron, "Jerry's skipper, Freddy's crew, and I'm passenger." He settled himself on a cushion amidships. "I'm not going to do anything but enjoy myself."

Freddy and I raised the sail. I took the tiller and the sheet. Freddy cast off. We waved to Aunt Edith, who stood on the road watching us, and she waved back. We beat our way down the river in a series of short tacks, but once we got into Sewell Harbor we had wind and water to spare. I pointed the catboat in the general direction of Houghton Landing. To port, Gull Neck stuck out of the marsh like a pointing finger and extended south for eight sandy, scrubby miles until it terminated in a pile of rocks topped by Gull Point Light and the Coast Guard station. Gull Neck served Sewell Harbor as a breakwater against the open Atlantic, and Gull Ledges, a series of sandbars studded with rocks extending into the harbor from about the midpoint of Gull Neck, were the only hazard to sailing there. Most of the time they were out of water, and sometimes we went to them to look for the big sea clams that lay around on top of the sand and were especially good for chowder. For about an hour before and after high tide the ledges were underwater and a hazard, but they were marked with a black marker. You had to be very ignorant or very stupid to run aground on them.

To sail to Houghton Landing, you coasted inside Gull Neck, skirting the ledges, until you came abreast of Gull Point Light. From there you took a south southeasterly course for about five miles of open ocean until you came under the lee of Houghton Heights and into the landing. The catboat nipped along on a reach with a steady east wind coming over the port side. I figured that with such a steady wind we'd burn up the five miles of open ocean between Gull Point Light and Houghton Heights. We had time to sail to Houghton Landing, buy ice-cream cones and be back at the cove in time to swim before supper. I had made this trip often with Grandma, starting when I was a very little girl and the purchase of an ice-cream cone was a big occasion for me. The ice-cream sail, as I privately called it, still excited me. (It does today in 1944. If we only had a sailboat, how I'd love to bundle the little boys in life jackets and take them on an ice-cream sail, the way Grandma used to take me.)

"Let's sail to Houghton Landing and buy ice-cream cones," I said to Bron and Freddy. "That is, if anyone has any money."

Freddy had a nickel in his pocket, and Bron found twenty-five cents in his, which was just enough. We settled down for an afternoon's sail.

"There are some questions I want to ask you and Freddy," said Bron. "This is a good chance." He stretched out his legs. "First I've got to tell you about the afternoon before your grandmother died." And he told us in a general way what Aunt Edith has already described in detail in her narrative.

"I can't forget," said Bron, "how hard she tried to tell us about that quilt, and we would have found it for her, too, if Deadeye Dick hadn't interfered. Well" — he looked inquiringly from Freddy to me — "did she ever say anything to either of you about a special quilt that was hidden somewhere?"

Freddy shook his head, but I remembered.

"There was a quilt. She said it was ugly as sin."

"Aha!" cried Bron. "Tell me about it."

"She showed it to me last summer. She said that the year after Henry Hardin robbed the safe, she sulked in her room and pieced the quilt. It *was* ugly as sin, too." I fixed my eyes on Bron and shuddered. I wanted him to realize how ugly it was. "It makes me sort of sick just to remember it."

"Go on," urged Bron. "Did she say anything more?"

"Yes, she did, and I remember it because it wasn't like the things she usually said. She said, 'I must look at it sometimes to remind myself of my sin from which there is no escape.'"

Bron frowned and shook his head as if he could hardly believe what I had told him.

"You're luffing, Jerry," shouted Freddy, and added a little peevishly, "I don't see why you never told me about this."

I took in the sheet. "I never told anyone before. I don't like to remember it."

Bron continued to frown. "She told Edith and me, when we were young, about how she took to her room after Henry Hardin went off with all the money. She stayed there until her father died and she had to come out to support her mother and herself. She never mentioned a quilt to us. I'm sure Edy doesn't know anything about it either." He paused. "She must have kept it hidden somewhere. Do you know where?"

I shook my head. "She brought it into my room just when we'd finished making my bed. She shook it out to air it and we looked at it, and she said what I told you, and then she took it away out of my room again."

"And you've no idea where she went to get it, or to put it back?"

Again I shook my head.

"You're going to have to do better than that, Jerry," said Bron. "You must remember something that will give us a clue."

"No, honest I don't."

Bron sighed, then smiled at me. "I'm not going to let you off that easy. I'm going to try to make you remember more than you think you do. Change places with me and give me the tiller." I did as he told me. "Now," he went on when we were resettled, "stare at something that has no meaning or interest for you, like a rib or a plank in the bottom of the boat, and try as hard as you can to remember yourself back into that scene with your grandmother and the quilt. Try to remember every little thing — all the sights and sounds and smells that were around you and that you usually don't even notice because they are always there — and the weather and the time of day and what you'd had to eat, and all the little gestures or movements that you and your grandmother made as you did what you were doing, and what you were talking about — your exact words, if you can. As you remember the scene, tell it aloud to yourself, and don't leave anything out. Maybe I'll notice something that you've overlooked."

I didn't like giving up the tiller, or the idea of forcing myself to remember, but for Bron I was willing to try my best.

"We were in my bedroom at about nine in the morning," I began. "Honestly, Bron, I don't remember what I'd had for breakfast."

"Never mind," said Bron, and he urged me on with a nod and a smile.

"It was a warm, sunny day toward the end of last summer. I was helping Grandma to make my bed and mop and dust. I said I loved my room and the furniture and even the funny old books — though I didn't much care about reading them — but most of all I loved my shadow-and-sunlight quilt that Grandma had made especially for my bed. Grandma was bustling around with a dustcloth. She said she'd loved the room too when she was a girl and it had been hers. She ran her hand over the quilt — it has thirty-six hundred pieces in it — and she smiled, and I thought she looked proud.

"Suddenly she stopped smiling and looking proud. She gave me her dustcloth, and she said — I can't remember her words exactly — that there was another quilt she was going to show me. She told me to finish dusting while she went to get it. She went out and shut the door of my room behind her. It made a click and a thud. After that it was very quiet. I didn't hear Grandma's steps going off in any direction, but I guess that was because she was wearing her house slippers. I remember the smell of the dustcloth. I didn't like it. I went to the window to shake it out. At the window I smelled arborvitae and marsh and ocean and maybe the petunias around the flagpole — smells

I like. I wished Grandma would hurry up with her quilt so I could go out and play. I saw the wisteria vine spreading out over the top of the porch. I saw the marshes stretching way off to the ocean, and some sky with seagulls swooping around. They were screeching at each other, the way they always are, but they were far off and the screeching wasn't very loud, just a sort of rasping sound. I shook out the dustcloth and started wiping the window ledge, and I guess I was getting more and more impatient to go out because once I mistook the rasping noise the seagulls were making for the sound of my door opening. I jumped around, expecting to see Grandma coming in, but the door stayed shut. I started dusting my bureau . . ."

"Wait," Bron interrupted. "Are the hinges of your door rusty? Did they rasp when your grandmother went out the door and closed it?"

"I don't think so. I just remember a click and a thud."

"If your door hinges didn't rasp, why would you mistake the rasping of the seagulls for the rasping of the hinges?"

"I — I don't know. I was hoping the door would open and Grandma would come back, and that soon I could go out. The sound the seagulls were making reminded me of doors opening, I guess, and, well, I guess . . ."

Bron silenced me with a wave of his hand. "The seagulls were in front of you, far away, outside your window, and you think the rasping sound you heard behind you, inside the house, that reminded you of a door opening on rusty hinges, was made by the seagulls?"

"Well, yes, I did, Bron. At least, I think . . ."

"I've caught you, Jerry!" Bron's eyes glinted. "You fooled yourself then. You're fooling yourself now, but you can't fool me. Your hearing and sense of direction are both excellent, but seagulls aren't ventriloquists. What you heard *was* the rasping of rusty hinges somewhere inside the house." He grinned.

I just looked at him and shook my head to show I didn't understand.

"You've given me the clue," cried Bron.

"I have?"

Bron threw back his head and laughed. He looked terribly handsome with his chin lifted and his hair flying back and shining in the sun. I was happy that I had done what he wanted me to, even though I wasn't just sure what it was or how I had done it, or whether or not he was laughing at me.

"I thought we should look there, and I told Edy so," exclaimed Bron, "but she said her mother would never hide anything she valued up there. It never occurred to either of us that she didn't value it, that she hated or feared it. Why? I wonder why." Bron's forehead puckered, he stared off at nothing and forgot he was sailing a boat. I grabbed the tiller and swung us into the wind just in time to avert an accidental jibe.

"Thanks," said Bron, coming to. "We'll go right back and find it. Won't Edy be surprised!"

Freddy turned from his forward station. "I wish, Bron, you'd tell me where the quilt is hidden. I still don't know."

Bron chuckled and smiled at Freddy. Freddy always had a gentling effect on people, and I was glad he had asked. If I'd had to ask, Bron might have thought I was dumb.

"The quilt is in the cupola on top of The Haven, Fred. What Jerry heard were the hinges of that old roll-up ladder rasping. They must be rusty as anything. Your grandmother never allowed anyone up in the cupola."

"Can we climb the ladder and go up in the cupola with you, Bron, when you go up to get the quilt?"

"Sure."

"Oh, boy!" cried Freddy. "That's been one of my life ambitions."

"Mine, too," shouted Bron. "Ready about, hard alee." And he brought the catboat about with a jerk. He had forgotten our ice-cream sail, and he didn't seem to notice that the wind was rising and that strong gusts were hitting us abeam. He kept the sheet taut, even when the catboat heeled so that she took water over the lee side. I would never have dared to sail so close to the wind in gusts like that. Freddy and I sat as far out as we could over the windward gunwale. We were a little scared and we got soaked, but just the same, it was fun.

When we got back into the river out of the wind, we hardly seemed to be moving, and Bron made me paddle to hurry us along. After we had tied up in the cove, we almost capsized the skiff, we were in such a hurry to get in it and get off. We even forgot all our gear and left it on board.

Edith's Narrative

The Crazy Quilt

I HAD JUST GOT HOME with my books and was sitting on the side porch for a minute before going inside to look in on Father in his study, feed Sunbeam, and start supper. Bron and the children hit me like a cyclone. First they were too breathless to say anything, then they all shouted at once. It was some time before I could make head or tail of what they were trying to tell me. Then I thought it very strange that Mother had shown an unusual quilt to Jerusha when she had never so much as mentioned it to me.

I made Jerusha repeat the story to me as quietly as she could — not that I questioned the child's truthfulness: though excited and woefully inarticulate (a year of Latin with me, I thought, would improve her diction), Jerusha was not making anything up. Freddy kept interrupting her and begging me to get up and look. He and Bron tried to haul me out of my chair. I refused to budge until they all quieted down. The last thing we wanted was to alarm Father so that he came out of his study. I begged them to step lightly and led them up the stairs to the central hall.

I unhitched the rope from its cleat in the wall. The levers squeaked, the hinges rasped, and the ladder swung slowly down, along with a shower of dust. Bron and Freddy were poised to swarm up, but we all caught our breath and stopped still when we saw the unmistakable prints of Mother's old house slippers in the dust on the steps. It was as though her ghost had passed among us. Jerusha sobbed and ran to her room. Freddy fell back and took my hand. Slowly Bron climbed the ladder, pushed open the trap and climbed on up into the cupola. I heard the gurgling and flapping of disturbed pigeons and a grunt of disgust from Bron. He came down quickly, carrying an old tin box.

"If you still want to go up," he said to Freddy, "go now before those filthy birds get back."

Freddy squared his shoulders, climbed the ladder, disappeared through the trap door, reappeared, and scrambled back down the ladder.

"Holy cow!" He held his nose and rolled his eyes, and made retching noises.

"That will do," I said.

Bron carried the box to the head of the front stairs where the light was good. I got a rag and wiped it off before I let him set it down on Grandfather Haskell's camphor chest.

The quilt, when I'd lifted it from the box, unfolded it, and spread it over the chest, was every bit as ugly as Jerusha had said. Properly speaking, it wasn't a quilt at all, for it was neither lined, nor backed, nor quilted. It was just the patched

top for a crazy quilt. The patches, whether printed or solid, were for the most part brownish, slimy green, or purple. They were stitched together sometimes with red and sometimes with black thread. A few solid black pieces scattered among the others looked disturbingly like black holes outlined in blood. When I forced myself to examine the workmanship closely (the uncouthness of the overall design repelled me), I was further distressed by the sloppiness of the sewing. In some places Mother had even used double thread, like a child who is just learning to sew. Freddy put his arms around me and buried his face in my skirt. I hugged him and told him to forget the ugly quilt, get Jerusha, and take her outside to play until supper.

As I looked at the quilt, I could imagine how, as a young woman, deeply hurt, my mother might have given vent to her misery in this abominable piece of needlework, but I could not understand why my mother as I had always known her — an exquisite needlewoman with good taste, good sense, and good humor — had kept the thing. Did she really believe that falling in love with Henry Hardin (as I was pretty sure she had) was a sin for which she must go on punishing herself till the day of her death? I doubted it. Yet, I had heard Jerusha's story, and there was the quilt in front of me. Bron had been staring at it as if mesmerized.

"Can this be what she wanted?" I asked him.

"I think so. She pointed up, in the direction of the cupola."

"I'm glad we didn't find it in time," I said. "It could only have made her more miserable." I took Bron's hand. I felt the need of his warmth and strength. "Let's get rid of it. Let's burn it. It's disgusting."

"Not yet." Bron squeezed my hand — a little absently, I

thought. "There is something puzzling about it, quite apart from its ugliness. It reminds me of something it shouldn't have anything to do with. I don't know what. I need to study it."

A yowl rose from the foot of the stairs, followed by Father's voice — rich, beautiful, and querulous. "Edith, Edith, where are you?"

Quickly Bron picked up the quilt, folded it, and put it inside the chest.

"Right here, Father. I'm just coming down."

"Sunbeam won't let me work on my sermon. He jumps on my desk. He waves his tail in my face. He sits on my paper. He rubs his cheek against mine and purrs in my ear. The attention is flattering, but I cannot work, and I believe the poor fellow is hungry. Edith, are you listening? I believe he wants his supper, and with good reason, too, because it is late, and as a matter of fact, I am hungry, too. Edith," Father's voice rose, "why are you up there and not in the kitchen getting our supper? We have looked all over the house for you."

"I'm coming, Father, right away. Will you stay?" I asked Bron.

"Yes, thank you," said Bron. "I hope we can talk more about this later."

Visitors

Bron and I had no chance to talk because our first guests arrived before I had even finished the dishes. They were Chester

Bates and his mother. Chester picked Mrs. Bates up every night when she got through at Cousin Harriet's. Tonight he brought her over to see the children and visit with Father and me while he put the recharged battery in the Electric. In spite of the string on his finger, Father had forgotten to stop at the garage.

I always liked to see Chester and his mother together. He is a burly six foot four, and she was barely five feet and about as substantial as a grasshopper. Chester beamed down on her like an enormous, genial sun, and in the warmth of his smile, she hopped and chirped as gaily as if she really were a grasshopper, not a frail and elderly widow of very slender means. The Bateses, mother and son, were all that was left of one of Sewell's old and once-distinguished seafaring families. When Chester first started coming to see me, Mother took advantage of his visits to inspire him with ambition and a thirst for culture. She told him stories of the glorious past, as she had Bron and me. She tried to lend him books and magazines of an educational nature and she made him very uncomfortable, for though he was sensible and intelligent, Chester's ambition was to lead a quiet, useful life with plenty of time for tinkering with machines in general and electric wires in particular. He was very happy running his garage and serving on the police force (he had recently been promoted to chief). In his honest perplexity and rumbling voice, he had stated his feelings to Mother.

"Mrs. Faunce, next to my own mother I respect you more than any other woman. In my opinion, Reverend Faunce is the kindest man in the world and Edy is the most beautiful girl. I like to come to your house. I like to work on your Electric. There aren't too many around these days. I enjoy putting in a switch or a wall plug where it's needed, and, if I say it myself, I'm the only man in town who understands your wiring. I'd drive Edy anywhere, day or night, if she asked me, and consider it an honor. I'd teach her to drive the Hup if she really wanted to learn. Edy does something for a car when she's in it. Even if it's just an old flivver, she makes it look sort of classy. But please, Mrs. Faunce, if you want to do me a good turn and don't mind my coming up here, please stop lending me history books. I can't get through them. I've tried. They just make me feel sort of guilty."

Now, after we had all greeted each other and the Bateses had expressed their pleasure at seeing the children again, Chester said, "I'm happy to bring up the Reverend's battery, and after I've put it in, I'll just check over the wiring in the stable. That will give Ma time to visit. Ma's a great one for visiting."

The Bateses exchanged glances of love and mutual admiration. "Ma never gets tired," Chester went on. "She works all day and at night she makes me take her visiting to tire her out so she can sleep." Chester chuckled. Mrs. Bates chirped delightedly and hopped into the rocking chair Father placed for her. Bron and the children followed Chester to the stable. He was a great favorite with all of them. Mrs. Bates rocked vigorously while she enumerated for Father and me all the potholders, aprons, and bibs she had sewed, the dishcloths, washcloths, and needlecases she had tatted, and the baby bonnets, sweaters, and booties she had knit for the July 4th bazaar.

"I know you are tireless," I exclaimed, "but I don't see how even you, Mrs. Bates, can do all that fancywork and still keep house for Cousin Harriet."

Mrs. Bates edged forward in her chair. "I'd go crazy without my fancywork. There's not enough to do over there" — she nodded in the general direction of Cousin Harriet's cottage — "to keep one able-bodied woman busy, let alone two. I told her so, right out. I said, 'You don't need me more than once a week.' She said, 'I like someone to be in the house when I'm not. On account of Miss Mary.' Money's no object with her, and strictly between you and me and the bedpost" — Mrs. Bates cupped her hand around her mouth and leaned even farther out of her chair — "that Mary is a handful, and sassy too. The things she says to her grandma! I'd like to take her right over my knee."

The screen door swung open, slammed shut, and Mary herself stood before us. She was swathed in black satin pajamas, skintight except below the knees, where the legs flared out into bell bottoms, and below the elbows, where the sleeves also flared and hung in folds around Mary's wrists. In an orgy scene from one of the new movie spectaculars like *The Sheik* or *Ben Hur,* Mary might have passed as one of the crowd. On our side porch in Sewell she was literally stunning. Mrs. Bates fell right out of her chair and had to climb back in. I was speechless.

Father recovered first. "You must have lost your way, my dear young lady," he said, rising politely. "The costume party is not here."

Mary gave a shriek of laughter and smothered it in one of her sleeves. "He's a scream," she whispered aside. "He doesn't know who I am."

"Mercy," gasped Mrs. Bates, back in her chair and rocking and fanning herself as if she needed all the air there was, and then some. "Has your grandmother seen you?"

"Of course not." Mary turned impatiently to me. "I'm

looking for Bron. I went to the cove, but he wasn't there. I thought maybe he was here."

I was about to reply that she could find him in the stable, when I heard footsteps outside. The screen swung open again, and in marched Cousin Harriet.

"Good evening, Wilfred and Edith," she trumpeted. "You will be happy to know that I have brought my tenants, the Munsons, to meet you." With a sweep of her arm she waved in the Munsons, who hesitated at the door. With her arm raised, Cousin Harriet looked like a ringmaster introducing the next act. Her eye fell on Mary and she froze in that theatrical attitude.

Mary realized she was caught. "Oops," she cried, rolling her eyes and shaking all over in a parody of fear.

Cousin Harriet unfroze slowly. "What," she demanded, "are you doing in that rig?"

Mary gave a defiant toss of her head. "I'm looking for Bron Zebra, if you want to know."

"Bron Zebra?" repeated Cousin Harriet in a tone of mingled distaste and disbelief, as if she were saying "Al Capone," or "the Kaiser."

"Any objections?" demanded Mary, still pert.

Cousin Harriet's cold, old eyes traveled up Mary and down her. "Go home at once and take off that ridiculous costume and go to bed."

"It's not a costume. It's lounging pajamas. They're haute couture. In Hollywood, everyone wears them and I think they're the cat's meow."

Cousin Harriet made no reply, but went on looking Mary up and down. Mary faltered. "They're just lounging pajamas. I bought them this afternoon, after the show, while I was waiting for Mrs. Munson to pick me up." She appealed to Mrs. Munson. "Remember? I told you."

Mrs. Munson stepped forward. She was an attractive, competent-looking woman, still quite young. She shook her head at Mary, but her eyes were kindly.

"You didn't tell me what they were like or show them to me. If you had, I would have advised you to take them back."

"You mean you don't like them?"

"Not on you," said Mrs. Munson. "They're not becoming."

"Oh, gee." Mary seemed to shrink back into a little girl, and Father realized who she was.

"Poor little Mary," he said. "You must be cold in that funny black-cat costume. Edith, fetch her a sweater."

Mrs. Munson smiled at Mary. "Everyone makes mistakes in clothes. If you go home now and take them off we can change them for something more becoming tomorrow."

"Oh, gee. Well . . ." Mary started away, turned, and whispered earnestly in Mrs. Munson's ear. Mrs. Munson shook her head and gave Mary a gentle shove toward the door. "Okay," said Mary, "if that's what you think, I'll go home, but" — she tossed her head at her grandmother — "I won't go to bed." She ran off into the night.

"I hope she is fetching a sweater," said Father. "The nights here are damp."

For almost a minute Cousin Harriet glared at all of us, one by one, too affronted to speak. When her glare rested on Mrs. Bates, that lady glared back.

"A good spanking is what she needs," declared Mrs. Bates with a jerk of her whole diminutive frame. "If you can't do it yourself, I'll ask Chester to give it to her. She's spoiled rotten."

"When I need your advice, Mrs. Bates" — Cousin Harriet's formidable bosom swelled — "I'll ask for it."

"Please, dear Harriet," said Father, "introduce us to your charming young friends. I am afraid I did not catch their names."

Father, as I have said before, cannot say boo to a sheep. Neither can he hear others quarrel. His instinctive gentleness and good breeding, his courtly manner, his beautiful voice, quieted both ladies as I believe nothing else could have. Mrs. Bates retired into her rocker. Cousin Harriet's bosom deflated, and she made the proper introductions. Father and I found chairs for our new guests, and Cousin Harriet proceeded to tell Father how she proposed to use the Munsons and their products at the church bazaar. Mrs. Munson was to have a booth at which she would sell Dagmar cosmetics, and the difference between the retail and wholesale prices would go to the church. Furthermore, for a dollar, Mrs. Munson would make people up, showing them how to use Dagmar to the best advantage. All the dollars she earned in this way were to go to the church. Cousin Harriet herself would decorate the booth and help with the selling. While Cousin Harriet blared on and on to Father, Mr. Munson engaged Mrs. Bates in conversation, and Mrs. Munson spoke to me.

"I think the booth will be successful. Women are interested to learn that make-up needn't be cheap and conspicuous. Properly used, it is both inconspicuous and becoming. Mary, for instance, has learned to use make-up cleverly." Mrs. Munson smiled. "So far, though, I haven't done much toward improving her taste in dress."

I agreed that Mary's lounging pajamas would be more appropriate in a harem than in Sewell.

"Poor Mary," said Mrs. Munson. "She dressed up to vamp Mr. Zebra, à la Theda Bara. I blame myself for her behavior. You see, Mr. Zebra and I have worked out a sort of business arrangement. I tell the people I meet (and I meet a lot in my business) about his sightseeing and fishing trips, and after each trip he passes out samples of Dagmar sunburn cream. It may seem silly to you, but people like to get the samples and, when you're starting a business, every little bit helps. It's been a good arrangement — profitable to us both. When Mr. Zebra is in his boat, moored off the town wharf, or here at the cove, I've used Mary as a messenger. I can't swim myself, and I'm afraid to row. I have to send someone out, and Mary loves to do it. The exercise has been good for her, and I never dreamed she would get a crush on Mr. Zebra. I'm afraid if she goes on chasing him this way that I must speak to her. She is so ignorant, self-centered, and stubborn that it is hard to know how to approach her. Sometimes she makes me quite angry, but I try not to show it. After all, she is only a child." Mrs. Munson sighed.

"Well," she went on, "I didn't mean to discuss poor Mary, I did want to say that my husband and I hope, from now on, to be able to attend church regularly. Actually, it was I, not Mrs. Cornish, who suggested selling cosmetics at the bazaar. I want to do something to help."

I said that most of the people who came to Sewell for the summer weren't interested in our church affairs, and that we were especially grateful and happy when one of them did show some interest.

Mrs. Munson said that both she and her husband came from small Indiana towns where all social life centered around the church. She herself was a minister's daughter — one of twelve children. Her parents had been strict, poor, and bigoted. Her childhood, as she remembered it, was a struggle against poverty and sin, waged under the constant threat of hellfire. The church had been her refuge and her only source of happiness. The little, cramped building had seemed a palace to her. The wheeze of the organ had been heavenly music to her ears. The church fairs, socials, and picnics had provided the only fun she knew about. She sat quietly for a moment, looking at Father, who was still being courteously attentive to Cousin Harriet, and she sighed.

"If my own father had been a gentle man like Reverend Faunce," she said, "and if my home had had a little of the dignity of The Haven, I would never have left it. When I was eighteen, I ran away. I went to New York. I've been lucky, far luckier than I deserved. I don't regret that I left home, but sometimes I am homesick. My husband and I both dream of settling down in a small town."

I felt, from the way Mrs. Munson spoke, that she was neither trying to butter me up nor looking for compliments. I liked her honesty and sincerity, and I offered to show her the house.

We had risen and were about to go in when Chester, Bron, and the children came back from the stable and, simultaneously, a car drew up and stopped behind Chester's on the drive. A man in a white uniform stepped out and strode toward the porch. I did not recognize him and, assuming he had lost his way, excused myself to go out and give him directions. He halted in front of me, clicked his heels, and bowed.

"I hope you are well, Miss Faunce, and that Reverend Mr. Faunce is well, and that I am not intruding on a festive gathering."

"No," I said, "not at all. Some neighbors have dropped in."

I remembered him now, but I couldn't for the life of me think of his name.

"I am glad of that." He bowed again. "I have had it on my conscience ever since I was here over a month ago that I alarmed the Reverend Faunce when I spoke of how we of the Coast Guard plan to wipe out rumrunning here in Sewell. I have wanted to come again to reassure him, to set his fears at rest. Furthermore" — he gave me a significant look and a smile — "Jack Dawson isn't the man to forget a beautiful girl like you, Miss Faunce. No siree."

I was so relieved to have learned his name so easily that I must have asked him to come in with more enthusiasm than I felt.

"Edith," he said, "I hope you don't mind if I call you that. I've been thinking about you a lot. Believe you me I have. I guess maybe you were disappointed when I didn't come around again right away. Maybe you thought I'd forgotten you. I hadn't. No siree. The truth is I'm up to my ears in work and responsibility." He leaned close to me and went on in a loud whisper. "Things are going to be popping around here. You can bet your life they are! I jut sneaked out to come and tell you — and of course the Reverend — about our plans, so as not to alarm you."

"You're very kind, Lieutenant Dawson," I said. "Father is on the porch."

"Aw, c'mon," said the lieutenant, "call me Jack" — and he gave me a poke in the ribs.

"Very well, Jack," I said. "Come in."

He lingered and grinned. "I can see you've got a lot of company tonight, so I won't stay long, but another night, if I can get off, I'll come up and take you for a spin in the staff car.

It's a Stutz. Usually you've got to be a commander at least to
get to use a car like the Stutz, but I can take it any time."

"Because you are so important?"

"That's right. I don't expect you get to ride in a car like the
Stutz every day of the week. It'll be quite an experience for
you. I can't say when it will be, but don't worry" — he leered
at me — "I'll be 'round."

"It will be a surprise for me to look forward to," I said with
a lack of enthusiasm which Lieutenant Dawson should have
noticed but didn't.

I brought him onto the porch, introduced him to everyone
there, and seated him on the side of Father that wasn't already
taken by Cousin Harriet. Lieutenant Dawson set right to
work at his self-appointed task of reassuring Father by pre-
paring him for The Worst. He spoke more loudly than was
necessary — Father is not at all deaf — and he was obviously
gratified when everyone abandoned former conversations to
listen to him. (At the time, I found both his officious manner
and official jargon distasteful. I do not wish to reproduce
them now. I will give only the gist of what he said.)

Large boats sailed from Canadian, and sometimes West In-
dian and European ports, loaded with alcoholic beverages to
be sold in the United States in violation of the Volstead Act
of 1919. The boats coasted along just outside United States
territorial waters, where they could not be stopped and searched
by our Coast Guard patrols. The rumrunners on shore kept
in touch with these feeder or mother ships, as they were called,
by radio signal. At prearranged times, usually at night, the
rumrunners sailed out in small boats from harbors along the
coast, rendezvoused with the feeder ships, loaded up with liquor, and slipped back to their original ports or, more likely,

to remote coves or inlets. Here the cargo could be unloaded without attracting attention and dispatched by truck to the bootleggers who, in turn, distributed it (for a price) to thirsty Americans. To the Coast Guard fell the task of seizing the contraband liquor while it was being run in from the feeder ships to the trucks.

Lieutenant Dawson pointed out that the coast in the vicinity of Sewell, which he was assigned to cover, was ideal for rum-runners. It included large expanses of uninhabited wasteland and marsh, myriads of small, hidden harbors, and many rivers and inlets with treacherous currents and shifting sandbars which could only be navigated by men who knew them well. He cited our cove as a smuggler's haven, and poor Father interrupted to exclaim that our cove was neither treacherous nor shifting, and that it certainly wasn't hidden. Everyone in Sewell and adjoining towns knew exactly where it was. Lieutenant Dawson ignored Father's interruption and proceeded in his reassuring way.

Lieutenant Dawson had set about to learn his territory thoroughly, and he believed that now he knew Sewell Harbor and the waters around Houghton Landing better than any man alive. Bron raised an eyebrow at Chester, and Chester shrugged. The result of the lieutenant's thoroughness was that he had been able to persuade his superiors to give him two extra patrol boats of the latest design, and crews to man them. He described the design and equipment of his boats in detail but, since I've never taken much interest in boats and their engines, I didn't follow. Neither did Father. We were both impressed, though, to hear that each patrol boat carried two machine guns.

"Whatever for?" exclaimed Father.

"Your protection, sir," replied Lieutenant Dawson in a steely voice.

The patrols under the lieutenant's command would, within a day's time, be covering their assigned area twice as often and twice as thoroughly as they had before the acquisition of the new boats. They had orders to fire on any vessel which, on being hailed, did not immediately heave to and come alongside for inspection. Lieutenant Dawson planned to skipper one of the new boats himself whenever his many other duties allowed, and he looked forward to some quick action and quick results. He rubbed his hands and swept us with a keen nautical eye. His nautical eye could not miss Chester, looming near the door, and the sight of Chester reminded him to add a coda to his piece. The local police, under Chief Chester Bates, were co-operating with the Coast Guard. Extra men had been sworn into the police force to patrol the shores. These men were not in uniform, but were armed with rifles and had orders to shoot at any suspicious-looking boats, trucks, cars, wagons, or persons.

"I don't expect much shooting," muttered Chester.

"You are right, Chief Bates," said the lieutenant. "It will be a very slippery rumrunner who passes unscathed through the meshes of the net we have cast. Nevertheless, we expect you to stand by."

"Yes, sir," muttered Chester.

Cousin Harriet announced in her loudest voice that she was glad something was being done at last to enforce the law, and that she intended to buy a gun and shoot it at every suspicious person and every suspicious rustle of the shrubbery that came to her attention. Father begged her to be careful: she might shoot Sunbeam who constantly rustled about our hill on private business.

I heard Mr. Munson speak for the first time in a flat, but not unpleasant, midwestern drawl. He had come to Sewell Harbor, he said, to relax after the stresses of business, and he had been thinking of buying a little boat and doing some fishing. He had hoped Mr. Zebra would advise him about the kind of boat to buy and teach him to run it. After listening to Lieutenant Dawson, though, he was afraid to go out in a boat, let alone buy one, for fear of getting lost, running aground, or, worst of all, being taken for a rumrunner and shot at.

On land, he said, he wasn't much better off. He had always enjoyed exploring back roads in his car and walking along desolate stretches of shore, but now he was afraid to. He supposed, though, that if he sat on his porch and was careful not to make any noise which might alarm his neighbor, Mrs. Cornish, he would be reasonably safe. We all laughed. Even Cousin Harriet emitted one of her rare, resounding *ha-has*. Both the lieutenant and Bron went over to Mr. Munson. I heard them good-naturedly urging him to forget his fears, buy a boat, and fish. Lieutenant Dawson told him how to recognize the patrol boats, when and where to expect them, and how to respond to their challenge. Bron offered to show him some boats that were for sale and might interest him. Then they all three huddled together, talking and drawing diagrams on scraps of paper. I was surprised to see Bron and Mr. Munson getting on so well with the lieutenant. I thought perhaps he was less silly when he was talking shop with other men than when he was trying to impress a woman, or an audience.

Cousin Harriet had been dissuaded from buying a gun by Mrs. Munson and Father, and the three of them were back on the bazaar. At this point, I thought, Mother would have gone into the kitchen and come out with a pitcher of lemonade and a plate of her sugar cookies. I hadn't a lemon in the house. I felt even more inadequate when Chester asked me to ask Lieutenant Dawson to move his car so that Chester could take his mother home. Poor Mrs. Bates had been lost in her rocking chair for I didn't know how long, with no one to talk to, and I had forgotten her. Mother would never have done that.

While the Bateses and I were waiting in the driveway for Lieutenant Dawson to back out his car, Chester remarked, "If you ask me, Lieutenant Dawson scared poor Reverend Faunce more than anything. Maybe he's right to warn people what to expect, but, as a policeman, I like to work quietly." He lifted his mother bodily into the front seat of the car while she giggled like a girl. Chester got in beside her and snapped on his headlights. "That reminds me," he said. "I'll be up next week to put a wall switch in your stable. It'll save the Reverend fumbling around in the dark for the pull-cord and maybe falling and hurting himself. I think I can rig a better antenna for his radio, too. It'll cut down the static." Chester smiled and nodded to himself. I hadn't the heart to tell him that Father preferred static to anything else that came out of his radio. "That Freddy's got all his buttons," Chester went on. "I'm going to show him how to make a crystal set." He started his motor. "I'll be seeing you." Mrs. Bates smiled, nodded, and bobbing up and down, waved as they backed down the drive.

Chester's car was no sooner gone than another set of headlights beamed up over the brow of the hill and Dick's flivver turned into our drive. Lieutenant Dawson had left his car at the side of the road and he walked back up the drive just behind Dick. He and Dick, who had met before, shook hands and we all went back to the porch together. I introduced Dick to the Munsons, Lieutenant Dawson was reabsorbed into the conversation with Bron and Mr. Munson, and Cousin Harriet pounced on Dick. She wanted to tell him about her rheumatism. Relieved of Cousin Harriet, Father first nodded, then dozed. Mrs. Munson signaled her husband that they should leave, but Mr. Munson, deep in conversation with Bron and the lieutenant, didn't see the signals. Cousin Harriet described her symptoms in full voice and detail. Suddenly Dick jumped up.

"Come to my office any weekday between two and four, and I'll see what I can do," he said. Turning to Father, he wakened him with a gentle pat on the shoulder. He announced to the company in general that Mr. Faunce was tired and that, as his doctor, he was ordering him to bed. Mr. Faunce would sleep better, he added, if the house was quiet. He didn't give Father a chance to make excuses or say good night, but led him off to bed. Mrs. Munson immediately collected Mr. Munson and Cousin Harriet and started them for home. Bron and Lieutenant Dawson, still pursuing their conversation, left a few minutes later. I remembered the unfinished dishes and went into the kitchen to wash them.

Dick came into the kitchen grinning. "I guess I got rid of them in short order. I don't see how you stand all that company hanging around half the night. I never get to see you. People ought to be more considerate, especially when you have the children here, too."

The children! I almost dropped the plate I was washing. I had forgotten all about them. I ran upstairs. At the door to Freddy's room I leaned against the frame to steady myself. My heart was pounding and my knees were shaking so that

I thought I might fall down. I turned the doorknob, shoved the door half open, and looked inside. Freddy lay fast asleep in his bed, nicely tucked in, with his quilt laid out ready to pull up if he felt cold. His window was open exactly two inches at the top, which was the way Mother believed windows should be at night. I tiptoed in, kissed his forehead, and tiptoed out again. A light shone from under Jerusha's door. I tapped and waited till she called, "Come in." She was sitting up in bed reading the detective story I had brought for myself, along with the geometry books, from the library. I have always liked detective stories, especially when I can't sleep at night. Jerusha gave me an inquiring and, I thought, rather hostile stare.

"I came to say good night," I said, "and to thank you for putting Freddy to bed. I'm afraid I forgot about you both."

"That's all right," replied Jerusha. "The main reason I came here this summer was to look after Freddy when you didn't."

I had wanted to tell Jerusha how, as I raced upstairs, terrible visions had raced through my head. She and Freddy had gone for a moonlight swim and drowned! She and Freddy had gone for a moonlight sail and capsized or been machine-gunned down by a Coast Guard patrol! I had wanted to sit on her bed and exclaim about my fright, and maybe rest a little, and chat a little before I went away. Jerusha's manner to me, however, didn't encourage intimacy.

"Well, good night," I said.

"Good night," said Jerusha. "I hope you don't mind my reading this. I found it under the geometry books in your bag."

"No, of course not." I felt that she was accusing me of

something — duplicity perhaps. "As long as it doesn't frighten you."

"Don't worry," said Jerusha.

I felt I had been dismissed, and I left.

Downstairs, Dick had finished the dishes and was waiting for me. "Come sit on the porch a minute and look at the moonlight through the wisteria. I bet you've been too busy all evening to notice it."

I admitted that this was true. Except as it figured in my terrors about the children, I hadn't noticed the moon, though I must have been vaguely aware of it. I was very tired. Dick sat beside me on the hammock and took my hand.

"Why don't you let me share your responsibilities, Edith? Why do you insist on going it alone?"

I replied, as I had many times before, that I had been brought up and educated to be self-reliant and self-supporting, and that I felt I was equal to doing what I believed was my duty both to my family and to my profession. Dick pictured for my benefit, as he had many times before, the rosy married life he and I might lead together. Freed from household drudgery (we could afford help), I could take better care of Father, and I might teach or study if I liked, too. Dick had no old-fashioned notions about woman's place being in the home. He would have an office in Houghton as well as in Sewell and, inspired by me, would become the best-known, most respected, and richest doctor in the area. We could, if I wished, restore The Haven to its original glory, and with Father, as long as he lived, and our children, we would live there happily forever after. Dick's ambitions meshed with my own, but I could only tell him, again, as gently as possible, that, though I liked and respected him, I didn't love him and couldn't marry him. I was too polite to say that I was terribly tired and wished he would go home. He finally left, glum but still not convinced that I meant what I said.

I Do My Best

DURING THE NEXT TEN DAYS I was too busy with preparations for the church bazaar and supper to think about anything else. My official job was to recruit waitresses, but, as my mother's daughter and, in a way, successor, I got all the jobs that had been shirked or forgotten or bungled by someone else. I remembered how busy Mother had always been before a big church affair, but she enjoyed the people and the bustle more than I did. I am afraid I felt a little superior to the local women with their gossip, squabbles, hurt feelings, sulks, and tantrums. Mrs. Munson (unlike most of the others) managed both Cousin Harriet and her booth with good nature and efficiency. I was grateful to her. I couldn't have kept my patience with Cousin Harriet along with all the others who pestered me.

I ended up by being grateful to Jerusha too. I had expected she would want to go out with me every day and get acquainted with some of the girls in the parish who would be helping their mothers. Not so. She wanted to stay at The Haven, sail, and look after Father and Freddy. She washed up after breakfast, cooked lunch when I couldn't get home, and usually washed the lunch dishes too. Her washings up were not very thorough, but I didn't criticize. I felt that for a girl of her age and impractical nature she did very well.

Dear Freddy! What a joy he was! When I came in the door, he always rushed at me, hugged me, and after a preliminary "Guess what?" told me everything he had done during the day. Between them, he and Chester put the new electric switch in the barn, rigged a new aerial for Father's radio, and built a crystal set for Freddy. I was glad to have Freddy work with Chester and learn from him. I was glad too that Freddy swam every afternoon with Bron and Jerusha. I felt then, and I still do, that children who spend their winters in unhealthy climates like Chicago's or London's need all the wholesome exercise and sun they can get during the summer. Unfortunately, once the crystal set was built Freddy spent time listening to baseball scores and cheap comedians on the radio. He never looked into a book. I determined, as soon as the bazaar was over, to read to him and try to interest him in some good books.

Bron was as busy as I during the day, for the weather was unusually fine and the summer season in full swing. Evenings he was not so busy as he had been. The summer people had evidently found more exciting kinds of night life than moonlight sails and fishing trips. Bron came to supper every night, and he was more like his old affectionate, enthusiastic self than he had been all summer. He made Father very happy by sitting and chatting with him after supper.

He also encouraged Father to spend an unconscionable amount of money on fireworks to set off privately, as was our custom, on the night of July third. Mother had initiated the custom long ago to give Father, who all his life has retained a small boy's passion for fireworks, a chance to set some off himself. At the public display he was never allowed to help out. He was considered too dignified and, I suspect, too impractical. Bron contributed money to our private fireworks too, and I didn't approve of that any more than I did of Father's extravagance.

I held my tongue, though. I told myself that any amount spent to cheer up Father was well spent. Also, I didn't want to spoil the general peace or my reestablished friendship with Bron. He and I spent our evenings happily together reviewing my geometry or, since Bron couldn't put it out of his mind, reviewing Jerusha's story of the quilt. He would bring the ugly thing down to the parlor to inspect it under the light. Then he would stare at it fixedly or glance at it suddenly from the corner of his eye, or over his shoulder, or from other peculiar angles. I think he hoped some hidden figure would pop into view like the rabbit or kitten that lurks in the foliage in picture puzzles for children. When Dick came, as he sometimes did after evening office hours, Bron bundled the quilt away but stayed on himself and went out of his way to be pleasant to Dick. He seemed to be trying to make up for his former rudeness, and this made me happy. I hated their quarrels. Also, when Bron stayed with us, Dick didn't try to persuade me to marry him. Neither Chester nor Lieutenant Dawson put in an appearance. I suppose they were too busy patrolling.

On the eve of the Fourth, Father and Freddy were so excited about their fireworks that they could hardly eat supper, and after supper, of course, they could hardly wait for it to get dark enough to begin. I might have lost patience and scolded them both if Bron hadn't diverted us all by tuning in to some dance music on Father's radio. The music was so raucous it was hard to tell it from the static, but it had a catchy beat and Bron had us dancing to get in practice for the big shindig, as he called it, on the Fourth. He had already begged me, as if his life depended on it, to save three dances for him, and I had promised. The combined music and static inspired each of us in a different fashion. Father chose to waltz. Freddy did a solemn box step. Bron whirled and leaped like a cossack and carried me with him. Jerusha pivoted wildly from one foot to the other, slapping her knees and jerking her head in what she said was the Charleston. As we cavorted around the parlor, I felt gayer than I had since before Mother died.

Suddenly it was dark. Father and Freddy dashed out to start the fireworks. The first rocket misfired and headed for Cousin Harriet's cottage instead of the sky. She marched out to protest, but stayed on to watch. I went myself to invite the Munsons and Mary over. We brought chairs out onto the lawn, and Bron provided each of us with a lighted stick of punk to discourage mosquitoes. Dick turned up. He and Bron sat on the sidelines, and although I knew they both were itching to set off a few rockets themselves, they didn't interfere. Father's and Freddy's punk sticks darted about like fireflies as they chased here and there choosing rockets and Roman candles and setting them in place. "Ready," they cried on a rising pitch, "get set," and on "go!" their voices cracked with excitement. As each rocket soared upward they whooped, for all the world like a pair of wild Indians. In the light of the bursting bombs and flares, we could see the two of them jumping up and down and hugging each other. Such enthusiasm was irresistible. As each rocket rose, Cousin Harriet sucked in her breath, and at the boom of the explosion she exhaled in a sort of *moo,* which she sustained on a gradually descending scale until the last sparks had glissaded down and vanished. Then she clapped her hands like a child.

This time I had lemons. After the display was over, Jerusha helped me make lemonade and pass it, along with some cookies, to our guests. We sat in the warm darkness — the usual east wind had not come up — sipping our lemonade, talking, and looking up at the real stars, which, now that our false stars had burned out, seemed unusually bright. All our guests, as they left, said what a beautiful and happy occasion it had been. Bron outstayed the others and saw Father and the children to bed.

Later, as he and I stood in the yard together, he said, "To-night was like the old days when we were children. It was magic. Even the lemonade and cookies were magic."

"Nonsense," I replied, "it was just ordinary lemonade, and the cookies were boughten, but I'm glad everyone, and especially Father, had a good time."

Bron seized both my hands. "Tomorrow night will be star-light and magic too, and you promised to give me at least three dances. Oh, Edy, I am so happy. You won't forget?"

"Of course I won't." I laughed. "I love to dance with you."

In his impulsive, foreign way, Bron pulled me to him, hugged me, swung me once around as if we were dancing, made an elaborate bow, then spun around and capered down the driveway, snapping his fingers, kicking up his heels, and whistling some catchy popular tune.

"Good-bye," I shouted, and he waved his hand, blew a kiss, and danced away.

I laughed again, and as I looked up at those brilliant stars I felt certain of beautiful weather, a successful bazaar, and a glorious shindig to top off the Glorious Fourth.

I should have remembered that the only predictable thing about our Sewell weather is its unpredictability and not counted on holding the bazaar out-of-doors. The Glorious Fourth dawned raw, gray, and drizzly, with fog over the sea. We had to work like dogs all morning to move the booths back into the parish house. Chester and Mr. Munson came to help. Without them the women could never have got their heavy tables moved or the scaffoldings for their decorations torn down and nailed up again. I tried to help where help was most needed, and I commandeered Jerusha and Freddy to run errands. Mrs. Munson, I noticed, had put Mary to work too. In spite of Cousin Harriet, who did nothing but shout contradictory orders in a loud voice, they got their booth set up and in order before anyone else.

By the grace of God, the bazaar opened on schedule at one o'clock. Since the supper and dance had been planned for indoors anyway, they were not a problem. The bad weather turned out to be something of a blessing in disguise. The summer people, with their water sports spoiled by the rain and fog, came to the bazaar as they never had before. Every booth was sold out. They came to the supper, too, in such crowds that we had to turn some away. At eight in the evening, the committee voted to cancel the fireworks because the fog, which had been creeping in all day, was so thick you couldn't have seen a rocket if it exploded right in your face. This was a great disappointment to the children, and I was glad again to have had such a lavish display of our own the night before. The fireworks were no financial loss since we didn't charge admission to them and they could be stored away for another year. On the other events we made more money than we had dared hope for.

During the first part of the dance I was in the kitchen helping the women clean up after the supper and trying, as Mother always had, to compliment each one for her contribution to the overall success. When I came to the parish house, the orchestra was banging away, the dance floor was crowded, and people were lined up along the walls watching. It took me quite a while to make sure that in all that crowd there was no one who was likely to ask me to dance. No Munsons, no Dick, no Chester, no Lieutenant Dawson, and no Bron. The Munsons I guessed were too tired to dance after working so hard all day. Dick, although he had said he hoped to come to the dance, was always liable to be called away on an emergency. Chester and the lieutenant must be out patrolling again. But where was Bron?

The night before, his gaiety and his seeming so anxious to dance with me had made me long to dance too, as I hadn't since I was in my teens. All through the hectic day, the thought of dancing with him had shone for me like the spot of sunlight at the end of the tunnel. I was disappointed and a little worried too because of the fog. I told myself that fog wasn't dangerous if a boat was equipped with charts and compasses and if the skipper knew what he was about. Bron had certainly equipped the *Irene* to the teeth, and he was a good seaman, and he knew our harbor and the adjoining waters by heart. The fog had simply delayed him. It could do him no harm. Besides, I went on reassuring myself, Bron was so choice of *Irene* that he'd rather spend the night anchored out in the harbor tooting his horn at one-minute intervals and miss his date with me than risk hurting her. Several young men — summer people — asked me to dance. I danced with them to pass the time, for I still hoped Bron might turn up, and to forget the worry that nagged me. I had danced several dances before I saw Jerusha and Freddy. They were sitting in a corner against the wall. Freddy

was asleep in Jerusha's lap and Jerusha, slumped over him, looked so rumpled, so weary, and so utterly miserable that I knew I must get them both home and to bed at once.

When she had waited table at supper Jerusha had looked neat, happy, even pretty, and I had been proud of her. Now I remembered, conscience-stricken, that she hardly knew any of our Sewell young people. Mary Cornish, her one friend, was not the sort to help another girl find partners. Mary was regaling a group of unappetizing boys — she must have met them at the yacht club — with a demonstration of the Charleston. Poor Jerusha was being a wallflower at her first dance. I excused myself from my partner and went to the children. I wanted to apologize to Jerusha for not introducing her to some partners, but I was afraid she might resent it. I suggested that I find Father and we all go home. To my surprise — Jerusha was always surprising or disappointing me in those days — she said in the most woebegone whisper, "Bron never came."

"He stood me up, too," I answered, trying to sound cheerful and unconcerned. "He must have been delayed by the fog, but don't worry about him. Likely as not he is tied up in the cove, now that it is too late for him to get to the dance."

Jerusha just sighed. I supposed she had counted on Bron to dance with her when no one her own age did. She was at a difficult stage, I told myself, as I went to find Father. I should try harder to understand her.

Father was happy to leave a little early. We woke Freddy and groped our way to the Electric. The fog was thicker than ever. After Father lost track of the road and ran the Electric onto someone's lawn, I took the tiller. Although I didn't drive much in those days, my eyes were sharper than his. I made Jerusha and Freddy lean out the windows and shout when they thought I was veering too close to either side of the road. On the low ground at the foot of our hill where the fog was thicker than anywhere else, I lost my bearings and very nearly drove right off the road into the cove. I was so worn out when I finally got us home that I fell asleep as soon as I got to bed, without help from any detective story and with only a passing thought for Bron.

Jerusha's Narrative

My First Dance

How well I remember waiting there in the parish house for Bron to come and dance with me. At first I craned my neck, got up, sat down, and swiveled around in my chair to see over or through the dancers and spot him as he came in. The fog, I told myself, had delayed him, but he would be along. He wouldn't let me down. Freddy came and sat beside me. He was chewing Juicy Fruit and offered me a piece. It smelled delicious, but I refused because I wanted to look elegant and grown-up for Bron. Freddy said he didn't see how anyone could think dancing was fun, keeled over sideways into my lap, and fell asleep. I couldn't get up or swivel anymore. I tried shutting my eyes, counting to one hundred, and expecting that, when I opened them, Bron would be striding toward me. I began to itch in places that were either impossible to reach or indelicate to scratch. The hall was hot. My dress stuck to the back of my chair and I could feel my skirt getting damp where

Freddy lay on it. Still, when my eyes were shut, the whiffs of perfume from passing dancers, or of ham and scalloped potatoes left over from supper, or of Freddy's gum, mixed with the music and restored my confidence. I was at a dance. I was well dressed and pretty. When I opened my eyes, there would be Bron come to dance with me.

When the Virginia Reel was announced I knew the dance must be half over, and I lost the heart to go on with my game. I was far too young and humble to feel indignant or resentful. I felt desolate and suddenly afraid. Had *Irene* collided with a big fishing boat or a big rumrunner and sunk? Was Bron swimming blindly in the fog? No, I told myself, *Irene* carries a compass, charts, a searchlight in addition to riding lights, and a foghorn. Bron is the best sailor anywhere around. He has been delayed by the fog, but nothing terrible has happened to him. The sight of Aunt Edith reeling merrily with a partner I had never seen before, and, as far as I could tell, not worried about Bron's absence, further allayed my fears for him, but it raised another doubt. Maybe Bron had just been fooling when he asked me to dance. Maybe he hadn't ever intended to come. After all, he was a Catholic, not a Congregationalist.

Aunt Edith was grown-up and clever. She had known right along that all his talk about dancing was just a joke. I was so young and stupid that I hadn't caught on. Mary was right about me. I was wholesome and dumb, and I hadn't any sex appeal. I shouldn't expect to understand Bron or to be noticed by him, or anyone else for that matter. Not that I cared for anyone else, but Mary was dancing, Aunt Edith was dancing — everyone was dancing, but no one had asked me. I gave myself up to despair. I ached in every part — head, stomach, arms, legs, and heart. After a while Aunt Edith came to take us home.

Blissful Days

U<small>P UNTIL THAT NIGHT</small> I had been happier at The Haven than
I'd dreamed I could be without Grandma. Starting from the
night I got one up on Aunt Edith by putting Freddy to bed
when she had forgotten, everything was wonderful. Freddy
and I swam with Bron every afternoon in the cove, and Bron
always came home with us to supper.

In the late afternoon I waited in the arborvitae forest to spot
Irene as soon as she came round the last bend in the river heading for her mooring in the cove. I had a good supply of gum
and candy to chew on while I waited, because Chester bought
Freddy whatever he asked for and Freddy shared it with me.
No one told Aunt Edith. I had a mystery story too while I
watched. The minute I spotted *Irene* I went to find Freddy.
We put on our bathing suits and zigzagged down our path to
the cove. Bron fooled with us in the water, and ducked us, and
raced us to the float. He coached Freddy in his crawl and me in
my back dives until he said we looked pretty good. After swimming, he asked us aboard *Irene* to dry off and have a sarsaparilla and cookies, and he let me get them from the cabin and
bring them up on a tray.

Irene's cabin was the neatest, coziest little room I have ever
been in. Bron said he could lie in his bunk and reach everything he could possibly want, and this was true. There even
was a tiny icebox set in between a tiny sink and a tiny stove.
After I'd got the sarsaparilla and cookies out of the icebox, I
always looked at the pictures Bron kept on his chest of drawers
and took a sniff of his after-shaving lotion. The pictures were
of his own mother and father, Grandma, Grandpa, Freddy and

me with our own parents when we were little, and a whole lot
of Aunt Edith from the time she was a little girl right up to
now. The smell of Bron's after-shaving lotion made me catch
my breath and sent prickles of delight up and down my spine.
(For years afterward, when I smelled that particular brand of
after-shaving lotion, I felt the catch of breath and the prickles
and remembered Bron and that happy time.)

We lounged around on the forward deck, sipping, nibbling,
and talking about whatever came into our heads. Sometimes
it was boats and sailing. Sometimes Freddy and I told Bron
about Mama and Daddy and school and our friends in Chicago.
Our stories reminded Bron of stories about the days when he
and Aunt Edith were little and played together. He spoke of
his parents, too, and of how different they were from ordinary
American people. He said that, although he loved all of us and
tried to think of us as his family and The Haven as his home,
he couldn't feel truly one of us. Always he remembered his
foreign parents and, very, very faintly, a few scenes in the
Polish village where he'd been born. As soon as he had money
for the trip, he was going to see his village again and find out
about his relatives there. He said he couldn't settle down until
he had done this. This wasn't all he felt he had to do. He had
to do something outstanding in his life, something splendid.
He must make amends to his parents for their long exile. He
must prove to himself and the world that, for all his foreign-
ness and his funny name, he could be a better American than
any of us. I wanted to tell him that for me, already, without
even trying, he was the most outstanding, splendid, and radiant
creature alive, but I was afraid he would think me silly. Freddy
said that as far as he was concerned Bron *was* a great American.
Chester and Thomas A. Edison were the only others who came

close to him, and Edison, though undeniably the greatest of the three, might not be as friendly and fun to be with or as generous with candy and sarsaparilla as Bron and Chester. Freddy worried, he said, because the telephone, telegraph, electric lights, and now the radio had already been invented. Freddy wanted to invent something himself when he grew up, and he was afraid there wouldn't be anything left.

One day while we were in this confiding mood, I confessed that I was worried because I hadn't any steadfast purpose. When I was sailing the catboat in a stiff breeze, I wanted to be a champion yachtsman. When I was practicing my jackknives, I wanted to be a champion diver. When I was by myself, day-dreaming, I wanted to be a great author because wonderful scenes, all in words, went through my head, but when I tried to write them down it was very hard and they turned out not to be so wonderful after all. When I saw Aunt Edith in the evening in one of her pretty summer dresses, laughing and talking with Bron about subjects I didn't understand, and look-ing so beautiful in the lamplight, I wanted to be educated and beautiful like her, but I wasn't beautiful to begin with, and I had a terrible time keeping my mind on my work in school, and I never got very good marks.

"Don't worry," said Freddy, "you can leave school when you're sixteen, and you may get better-looking, and anyway we all like you."

Bron put his arm around my shoulders and patted me. "Fred-dy's right," he said. "You get prettier all the time, and don't try to be like Edy. It's too hard. She can barely keep it up her-self, and you are better off the way you are. How can any of us be better off than we are here now, in the sun?" Neither Freddy nor I said anything. Bron still had his arm around my shoulders, but he was looking off over the river and the marshes. We knew he was talking to himself, not to us. "Why spoil this," he tapped my shoulder absently, "with worry about what's going to happen later? And yet" — he sighed — "I know I don't deserve it, and that it can't go on." He took his hand off my shoulder to rub his eyes. For a minute he sat with his head bent and his hand over his eyes, then he lifted his head, laughed, and asked me to run down and get some more cookies.

One afternoon we were disturbed by a whoop from the shore. Mary, in her red bathing suit, waded out through the shallow water, launched herself on her stomach and started to flail her way out toward *Irene*. For all her lessons, she still didn't swim very well. Bron jumped up and let a little rope ladder down over the side so Mary could climb aboard. She stood amidships, dripping and smiling mysteriously.

"Where's the note?" Bron asked her.

Mary gave him the Clara Bow eye bat and hip wiggle and went on smiling mysteriously.

"Come on," Bron tapped his hand on the gunwale. "Take it out of your bathing cap and give it to me."

Mary giggled. "There isn't any note."

"Didn't Mrs. Munson send you?"

Mary placed both hands on her left hip, tossed back her head, commenced to jiggle all over, and said huskily, as if she had crumbs in her throat, "I got a yen to see you, and I never resist a yen." She half closed her eyes and squinted up at Bron through her lashes. Bron gripped the gunwale and drew a deep breath.

"If you've no note from Mrs. Munson, then jump right back into the water and swim away."

"*They're* here." Mary abandoned the Clara Bow-isms to

point at us. Her voice rang high and clear. "Why shouldn't I be here too?"

"I invited them," said Bron. He looked straight into her eyes, and as she gazed up at him, the new Mary fell away, and there was "poor Mary," dripping and shivering. "It was just a joke," she whispered, and dropped her eyes.

I had never thought I would ever feel sorry for Mary, but I did then, and I wished Bron would say something kind to her. He didn't. With a jerk of his head he indicated that Mary was to jump into the water. Without another word, she climbed up on the gunwale, took hold of her nose, and jumped. Bron didn't wait to see if she got safely to shore. He said he was going to change and went down to the cabin. When he came up again, he was dressed in clean white ducks and a white shirt. He said it was time for us all to go back to The Haven. He was silent all the way home. He didn't begin to be himself again until Aunt Edith sat down with him on the side porch to shell peas for supper. I soon forgot Mary and her humiliation. In all the rest of that happy time I never gave her another thought.

My days were very busy. Aunt Edith left right after breakfast to work on the bazaar, and I kept house. I made the beds and washed the dishes and remembered to pour the dishwater on the wisteria vine. I learned to run the kitchen range and, when Aunt Edith couldn't make it home for lunch, I cooked lunch and cleaned up afterward. Even Aunt Edith said I did a good job. I wrote lots of letters to Daddy and Mama telling them what good care I was taking of Grandpa and Freddy and the house while Aunt Edith was away. I made Freddy write too, and I hoped sometime Aunt Edith would remind us to write home so I could tell her that we already had. Whenever I wasn't busy and there was a wind, I took out the catboat. Freddy was more interested in wires and engines than in sailing, and I didn't urge him to come with me. I could sail the cat perfectly well by myself. I beat up the harbor and came down on long reaches, getting as much speed out of the old cat as she could give and always watching for *Irene* on her way out to or back from her fishing and sightseeing trips. When I spotted her, I'd give chase or try to intercept her. Of course I couldn't really do either, she was much too fast, but if Bron wasn't in a hurry he'd slow down for me or change his course to meet me. Then we would fool around and show off for his passengers. I'd sail across *Irene*'s bow while she came at me full speed, and I'd just make it, or I'd sail right alongside, as if I were going to board her. Bron and I would shake hands over our respective gunwales without letting them touch, and I'd come about and swoop away. Sometimes he pretended to chase me, and I tacked and jibed wildly to wriggle away from him. What with my household duties, fooling around with Bron, and making sure to be home and ready to swim with him in the late afternoon, I never managed to get in an ice-cream sail to Houghton Landing. My life was just too full to fit in everything I wanted to do.

So that happy time — a week and a little more — had slipped by and, on the afternoon of July third, Bron and I sprawled as usual on *Irene*'s forward deck, drying off after our swim, drinking sarsaparilla and eating Lorna Doones. Freddy was off with Grandpa buying fireworks. The tide was high, the sky was cloudless, no wind blew. *Irene* floated in a shimmering blue silence as magical as the settings of my morning dream fantasies. Bron sat up, looked east over the flooded marshes to the sea, sniffed like a dog, squinted a minute into the sinking sun, and said, "I think we'll have another fine day. I think it will be a super-glorious Fourth." He grinned at me and, without standing up, made a comical bow. "Miss Jerusha, may I have the pleasure of a dance with you tomorrow night at the great Fourth of July church social?"

"Gee, Bron," I said, "I'd love to dance with you. But I never learned much at dancing school, and I can only do the Charleston by myself — as soon as I tried it with the other girls I got mixed up."

Bron laughed. "Forget the steps, Jerry, and just follow me. You'll dance like Terpsichore herself. Come, I'll show you."

He jumped to his feet and down into the cockpit and held out his arms. I jumped into them, and he twirled me 'round and 'round *Irene*'s motor while we both sang "Yes Sir, That's My Baby" until we collapsed breathless and laughing on a bench.

"You dance divinely," said Bron when he caught his breath. "You must give me two dances and if there is a Virginia Reel, I want that too."

"Thank you, Bron."

"No, no!" Bron leaped to his feet and made a deep bow with a flourish. "Thank *you*, lovely Terpsichore. And now," he added, "I must dress in my best to be worthy of Edy's supper and the Faunce Family Firework Festival." He disappeared, laughing, into the cabin.

My heart throbbed and my head spun. Dancing with Bron had been like nothing on earth. It had been like floating on a cloud of bliss, and he had asked me to dance again, tomorrow night. I was bursting and running over with happiness. When Bron emerged from the cabin with his hair slicked back, with a navy blue blazer over his white shirt and ducks, and smelling of his after-shaving lotion, I felt all woozy. For a minute I must have have been off my head because suddenly Bron was shouting at me to wake up and untie the skiff, or was I deaf?

"You must have been dreaming about those fireworks." He grinned as I scurried astern. "We're going to have the best ones tonight we've ever had, and we've got to help Edy with supper and to clean up afterward so she can enjoy them, too."

"Fireworks? Who cares about fireworks?" I thought as I untied the skiff and pulled it alongside.

Bron rubbed his hands. "Nothing lightens the heart and lifts the spirits like fireworks. Isn't it so, Jerry?"

"Yes, Bron," I said, and held the skiff steady for him to climb in. If Bron had said that nothing lightened the heart and lifted the spirits like castor oil and Latin grammar, I'd have agreed with him. Devoutly, reverently (because Bron was in it), I rowed the skiff ashore.

As soon as we'd beached the skiff, Bron said, "Edy must dance with me tomorrow, too. I've got to ask her quick before Deadeye Dick and all her other flames get ahead of me. Gosh, I hope I'm not too late. Come on." He zigzagged up the hill so fast that I couldn't keep up with him.

For the rest of the evening I floated around in a dream. Nothing seemed real except my own happiness. I wondered that no one noticed how different I was from my old self and from all other people who weren't lucky enough to be me. After the guests had left, I could hardly wait for the rest of the family to get through in the bathroom so I could start getting ready for the dance. I took a very thorough bath and washed my hair and tied up the ends in rags so they'd curl a little and not just hang. I smeared my face and neck with some cold cream that

I found in the medicine cabinet, and then I got in bed to mani-
cure my nails, but I fell asleep before I'd finished.

The next morning was so damp, I didn't dare take the curling
rags out of my hair because I knew that as soon as I did, it
would go straight. I tied up my head in a bandanna, and Aunt
Edith and Grandpa were in such a stew about having to move
the bazaar indoors that they never noticed. All morning at the
church, the ladies flapped around like chickens without their
heads, telling me to run somewhere to get something that wasn't
there or that they didn't need when I brought it. They scolded
at each other and me, and got red in the face, and a few even
cried. I didn't mind them. I had true happiness in my heart.
I felt sorry for them, with nothing more important to think
about than an old church bazaar.

I had a dollar to spend at the bazaar, and I couldn't decide
between a make-up by Mrs. Munson and a big sea-clam shell
with a picture of Gull Point painted on it and little periwinkle
shells glued in a border around the edge. It was the prettiest
thing I'd ever seen, and useful too for holding pins, and I
wanted, if I could bear to part with it, to give it to Mama for
a present when I went home. On the other hand, the girls who
got themselves made up by Mrs. Munson looked much prettier
after than before, and I did want to look my best when I danced
with Bron.

I skittered back and forth between the knickknack booth
and the Dagmar booth, unable to make up my mind and frightened that someone else was going to snap up the clamshell.
If Bron had been around I would have asked his advice, but he
never came.

Finally I asked Freddy. Freddy said I should buy the clamshell because it was enduring. As soon as I washed my face the make-up would all come off, and I'd have lost my dollar. I got the clamshell. I set it on my bureau when we all went home after the bazaar to change into our best clothes for the supper and dance. It was pretty and I loved it but, when I was in the bathroom examining my freckles in the mirror under the bright light, I wished I could have afforded to get them covered with make-up too.

I creamed my face again and washed the cream off and pinched my cheeks to make them pink. Back in my room, I took the rags out of my hair and brushed it for five minutes, which was what Mama said a lady should do every day, before I put on my best dress and hairband. My dress was blue voile with a wide, low sash of darker blue silk and a white lace bertha. The hairband matched the sash. I had white, ribbed, silk knee socks and black patent-leather pumps. They were the first real, grown-up pumps I'd ever had. Before this year I'd had little-girl strap shoes for best. Mama and I had both thought that my feet, though large, looked slender and lady-like and less clumpy in the pumps than they had in the strap shoes. Mama had said that the blue of the dress brought out the blue of my eyes and the freshness of my complexion. She said the bertha was becoming because it hid my scrawny shoulders and my lack of bosom. It would be a year or so, she said, before I'd look well in décolletage.

I wished Mama could see me now as I saw myself in my bedroom mirror. My hair fell in soft, shiny waves and my neck and face rose fragile and flowerlike (just as I'd read in books) out of the beautiful lace bertha. In the shaded light, my freckles hardly showed. I had no more regrets about the clamshell. When I went downstairs, Grandpa and Freddy and Aunt Edith all exclaimed at how nice I looked. I told them that they looked nice, too, which they did, especially Aunt Edith. While I waited table at the supper, several people told me I looked nice. Mrs. Munson stopped me as she was leaving to tell me how nice I looked and to ask me to tell Aunt Edith that the Dagmar booth had netted $125 for the church. Everyone smiled at me, and I smiled back because I was so happy.

Rumrunners

I WILL NOT RETELL how my happiness crumbled and collapsed during the dance. It cheered me up a little to learn from Aunt Edith that Bron had stood her up, too. I might not have much sex appeal, but he had meant to dance with me, and I wasn't too dumb to understand a joke. As we blundered home through the fog, the like of which I'd never been out in before, my fears for his safety came back and began to gnaw at me. How I hoped, and prayed even, that he really was safely moored in the cove. As we passed it, I was so busy straining through the murk to see some shadow of *Irene* that I never noticed when Aunt Edith headed the Electric across the road and straight for the water. Freddy warned her just in time.

Home at The Haven, I sat in my room and waited for the others to get to bed so I could go back to the cove and make sure that *Irene* was there. If she was, I could forget my long misery and fall gratefully and happily to sleep. If she wasn't, I didn't know what I'd do — wake Aunt Edith perhaps and make her call out the Coast Guard. I tried not to think about

that possibility. When all the lights were out and the only sound was the faint, regular hoot of the foghorn at Gull Point, I slipped down the stairs and out the side door. At The Haven doors were never locked. My pumps crunched in the gravel of the drive and clopped on the road as I started down it. The fog was so thick that I was afraid to try the secret zigzag path. I needed the feel of the road underfoot to keep me on course. I judged that I was about halfway to the turnoff to the cove when I heard sounds below me — some scrapings and a click. I paused a moment and went on slowly. A voice boomed up out of the blackness.

"Stop where you are or I'll shoot. There are more of us, and we're all armed."

I stopped and felt my hair rising on my scalp. I heard other men's voices muttering together. I knew what I had done. I had walked head-on into the rumrunners or, just as bad, into one of the police patrols with orders to shoot on sight. I tried to call out, "Please don't shoot; I'm just a little girl," but as in a nightmare, the sound wouldn't come. I heard footsteps, growing louder, coming closer. I thought I saw the beam of a flashlight probing into the fog. I bent down, pulled off my pumps (thank heavens they weren't the old Mary Janes with straps), and holding one in each hand, tiptoed carefully and silently back up the road. When our gateposts loomed into view I made for the soft, silent grass along the edge of the drive and ran for the side door. In my room, I leaned my head against the window frame and listened. Except for the hoot of the foghorn, all was silent. I undressed, crept into bed, and pulled the covers up over my head. My heart thumped, and I couldn't stop shivering for a long time, but finally I fell asleep.

When I came downstairs late next morning, Bron was sitting at the breakfast table with the rest of the family. As soon as he saw me, he jumped up.

"I came at seven o'clock to explain about last night and to apologize, but everyone was asleep."

Freddy interrupted. "I was first one up, and Bron and I made waffle batter, and I'm starting yours now, Jerry." With a flourish he turned on the waffle iron.

I said, "Thanks," to Freddy, and kept looking at Bron. I didn't notice at first that he was haggard and red-eyed, only that he was alive and before me. He said that at about five in the afternoon the fog had lifted some in the cove and he had decided to take *Irene* over to his mooring off the town wharf. From there it was just a short walk to and from the church. He was out of the river and well into the harbor when his engine began to sputter. He got a screwdriver and adjusted the fuel injection. The motor died. He started it again and fiddled around making adjustments until it sounded right. Meanwhile *Irene* had been drifting, and the fog had thickened up again. He couldn't see anything. He set *Irene* back on course as best he could and proceeded very slowly and carefully right bang onto Gull Ledges. He was stuck fast. The tide was about an hour out. He had to wait eleven hours before he could float *Irene* off. He said he was disgusted with himself. He wouldn't blame me if I never spoke to him again.

I was surprised that Bron had taken *Irene* out in such a fog, when he didn't have to, and even more surprised that he'd been so careless of her, but I didn't say so. I could tell that he felt pretty bad about it. I just said that I had missed him at the dance and worried about him, but none of that mattered as long as he was safe — which was true. Aunt Edith said she had been telling him the same thing for the past hour and she wished he would cheer up. Bron just sighed. He refused Freddy's offer of another waffle to make him feel better. Grandpa gave Sunbeam his cream and patted him and began shuffling around, looking for things he needed to take with him to the church. He gave Bron a pat, too, and urged him to go upstairs and have a nap.

"This is your home, Bron," he said. "Edith and Jerusha aren't haughty young ladies whom you've offended. They are part of your family. They're just glad that you are safe."

Bron jumped up, kissed Grandpa, and escorted him out to the stable. It was when he came back that I noticed how red his eyes were. I decided that, since Grandpa was gone, I could tell about my encounter with the man in the fog. It might cheer Bron up to know that by running aground he'd probably escaped being shot. Bron scolded me for going out in the middle of the night.

"It was a foolish and dangerous thing to do. I would have thought you had more sense. I hope you'll never do it again." He didn't seem a bit cheered, and his sharpness rather hurt my feelings.

Aunt Edith wasn't cross at all. She said, "I never thought the time would come when we couldn't wander safely around Haskell's Hill and the cove at any time — day or night — but I guess it has. Jerusha and Freddy, you mustn't wander off by yourselves at night, and for heaven's sake, don't tell any of this to your grandfather."

Chester arrived with a present of raspberries, the first from his bushes. The berries were so delicious that we all ate them right out of the basket and almost forgot to save out enough for Grandpa's lunch. Freddy cooked another waffle for Chester.

While Chester ate, Aunt Edith made me tell him about my adventure in the fog.

Chester wiped his mouth. "That was a first-rate waffle, Freddy. Might I trouble you to cook me another?" He turned to me. "There were no patrols of ours at this end of town, so it must have been the smugglers themselves that you heard. We were all down somewhere below Houghton Landing on a tip from Lieutenant Dawson. The fog was so thick we weren't sure where we were most of the time, and my boys were so jumpy I was afraid they'd shoot each other. Where were you?" He turned suddenly to Bron. Bron explained where he was.

"Well, of all the stupid things to do!" exploded Chester. "I'd have thought you were a better seaman than that, but you were lucky just the same. From now on you'd better always tie *Irene* up nights off the town wharf. The rumrunning boys are tough, and after this I'll be hanging around the cove too, and my boys are awfully anxious to pull their triggers. They haven't had much training. They'd shoot you for a rumrunner any time they got the chance."

Bron said he'd move *Irene* that very morning and keep her moored off the town wharf.

Chester started his second waffle. "The machine works okay." He smiled at Aunt Edith. "It cooks them nice and even. I got Ma one just like it. She's crazy about it."

"So are we." Aunt Edith smiled back at him. "All of us, and we all missed you last night. The supper was the best we've had in years, but the dance would have been more fun if you had been there."

Chester laid down his fork. "I don't question the law," he declared. "I just enforce it, but it seems to me there must be smarter ways of enforcing it than by playing blindman's buff.

The kids who run the stuff in from the feeder ships are all local boys. I even know some of their names, and I know they've got friends and relatives working for the Coast Guard who tip them off about where Lieutenant Dawson plans to strike in plenty of time for them to be somewhere else. I've tried to explain to the lieutenant that he shouldn't announce his orders for the day like he was on a battleship, but I can't make him understand.

"Oh, well." Chester shrugged, picked up his fork, and had a few more mouthfuls of waffle. "Say, by chance or luck, I catch some of the kids, red-handed, as they say," he demanded when he finished chewing. "What's accomplished? Nothing, absolutely nothing! A few kids get sent to jail. A few burlocks of booze get confiscated, maybe. The bootlegging business goes right on flourishing, and the crooks at the top buy yachts, and racing stables, and cities, and counties, and whole states. Nobody bothers them. Nobody dares to, except when another crook gets sore or jealous and they shoot each other up. I hate shooting." Chester banged down his fork. "The only way to enforce this prohibition law is to find the big crooks and convict them and put them in jail. What can I do? I've got ten men and a hundred miles of coast to patrol, and it's all honeycombed with dinky little harbors, and every little harbor has a regular spiderweb of little twisty roads leading off in all directions, and the lieutenant can't keep his mouth shut, and, I ask you, what can I do?" Chester glared at us all, fiercely for him, then he sighed.

"I won't complain anymore," he went on. "I'll do the best I can, but I hated missing that dance last night. I wanted to dance with you, Edy, and I'd promised Ma to do the polka with her. She was disappointed when I couldn't make it." Chester finished his waffle and seemed to feel better. "At any rate, nobody got hurt. I'm thankful for that." He sat back and smiled at Bron, who was looking glum as ever. "It may make you feel a little less stupid about spending last night on Gull Ledges to know that the lieutenant ran his two new patrol boats spang into each other." Chester tried unsuccessfully to suppress his smile. "The lieutenant asked me not to mention it, but everyone in town knows by now, so what's the difference?"

Bron smiled for the first time that morning. "Were the boats badly damaged?"

"Were they ever!" replied Chester. "And was the lieutenant's face ever red! I guess I shouldn't laugh over his misfortunes, but he's such a big-mouth." Chester wiped his mouth and rose to his feet. "Thank you for those waffles, Freddy. They were a treat. If you'd care to come to the garage with me, I've got some jobs there you could help me with." Freddy jumped up, ready to go. Bron said he would go too, to move *Irene*. "I'll be up with the raspberries for jam soon." Chester smiled tenderly at Aunt Edith and patted Sunbeam and me on our heads. "So long."

Waiting and Wondering

As CHESTER, FREDDY, AND BRON climbed into Chester's car, the sun, which had been valiantly burning off the last remnants of fog, slid under a cloud. An east wind sprang up. Starting right then, sunshine and warmth left my life, too.

For one thing, all through the rest of July we never had another stretch of fine, hot days. For another, Aunt Edith started cleaning house. She said she had neglected the housework while she worked on the bazaar. She said Grandma would never have let the place get so filthy and she was mortified. So she started scrubbing and polishing and taking up rugs and taking down curtains and piling up the chairs on the tables. She had got the house so stirred up that I couldn't be comfortable anywhere, and then Chester brought up two dozen boxes of raspberries for jam. The raspberries wouldn't keep, so Aunt Edith left the housecleaning where it was and started on the jam.

When Grandma made jam I always helped her. I picked over the berries, and she didn't mind how many I ate on the side. When the jam was seething in the big kettle, and she was putting out the fire that was burning in the saucepan of paraffin because she had let it get too hot, I would notice just in time that the jam was boiling over. I always saved the day. I helped her decide whether the gob of jam she dropped from a teaspoon into a glass of cold water formed a soft ball, which meant the jam was cooked just right, or a hard ball, which meant it was cooked too much, or no ball at all, which meant we should let it boil some more. We were never sure whether our jam would turn out leathery, runny, or perfect, but we had fun.

Aunt Edith made jam scientifically with scales, a stopwatch, and a thermometer. She was so cross and particular that I didn't want to help her. I stayed out of her way. I sailed the catboat up and down the harbor in all weathers. I dug clams. I practiced swan dives at the cove. When the sun shone, I lay under the arborvitae with my candy, gum, and book. There was no zest in any of it, for Bron had stopped coming.

From the day he moved *Irene* out of the cove, none of us ever saw him. Once or twice, when I was sailing, I saw *Irene* in the distance, but she never came close enough for me to hail her. In fact, she was always sailing away from me. I knew Bron was busy, and maybe he didn't see me, but I wondered.

No, it wasn't the weather, nor Aunt Edith with her house-cleaning and jam that spoiled the summer for me. It was the absence of Bron and the suspicion that he was avoiding us. The summer was spoiled for Aunt Edith, too, and for the same reasons. She cleaned house and boiled jam to keep from think-ing about Bron. She never told me this. I found it out grad-ually, bit by bit, and, in the same way, she found out how I was feeling.

At this time she started to read aloud to Freddy before he went to bed. She sat with him in the parlor (the evenings had turned chilly), and Grandpa listened, and so did I, as she started reading from *The Jungle Book*. I had read the stories loads of times already, and each time I loved them more. Especially, I loved to hear them read aloud. The resounding cadences of "Look well, look well, O Wolves," always made my spine tin-gle, and the whole book pulsed with changing rhythms as exciting as the stories themselves. Yet, even when I was listen-ing to Aunt Edith reading out of my favorite book (and she read well) I was also listening for Bron. When Aunt Edith stopped in midsentence, as if something outside the story had jarred her attention, Grandpa coughed impatiently, Freddy wiggled and whispered, "Go on," but I pricked up my ears and listened with her. Aunt Edith and I listened, and hoped, and waited together for Bron. All through the day we went right on at cross-purposes, but in the evening our thoughts flowed together.

At supper, before Kipling charmed him into forgetfulness, poor Grandpa always complained because *Irene* was no longer in the cove and Bron never came to meals with us anymore, and he wanted to know why. Aunt Edith made up reasons for *Irene*'s disappearance and Bron's neglect. We all were careful never to mention the bootleggers at the cove in front of Grandpa. When he and Freddy had gone to bed, it was a relief to Aunt Edith and me to admit that Bron's behavior perplexed and worried us, and even hurt our feelings. When no visitors came, we sat up late talking about Bron and sewing, just like two grown-up ladies.

"All our lives," said Aunt Edith, "Bron and I have been quarreling and making up. We've never been not speaking so long as this before, and, so far as I know, this time we haven't even quarreled. Sometimes," she went on, "I wonder if he has fallen in love with a beautiful summer girl at the yacht club and can't tear himself away from her long enough to come here."

I remembered that session with Mary on my first morning at The Haven. "According to Mary, all the girls at the yacht club are crazy about him and chasing after him. Of course, Mary's an awful liar. She admits it herself."

"I expect Mary's right," said Aunt Edith. "Why shouldn't the girls be crazy about Bron? He's handsome and clever and full of fun. And why wouldn't Bron fall in love with a rich, gay, pretty girl who was chasing him? It all seems quite natural."

We both stiffened a moment, listening to something that might have been steps at the side door, but was only the wind.

"If he was in love with some girl at the yacht club," I said, "maybe he wouldn't want you to know."

"Why do you think that, Jerusha?"

"He knows Grandma didn't approve of the sort of summer

people who belong to the yacht club, and you don't either. He'd
be ashamed."

For a long time Aunt Edith stitched away at her square of
patchwork and didn't say anything. We were trying to finish
a quilt called Young Man's Fancy that Grandma had been
working on when she died.

"Do you really think that Bron stays away because he is in
love with a girl he is ashamed to bring home?" she asked.

I shook my head. "I don't think so, because I don't think
he'd fall in love with a girl he was ashamed of, and if he wasn't
ashamed of her, he'd want to bring her home to show her to
us."

"Exactly," said Aunt Edith. "Bron was never sneaky, and I
must say, Jerusha, that for a girl of your age you have good
judgment and good sense. While I'm at it, I might as well air
all my silly, vulgar suspicions. Sometimes I wonder if Bron is
mixed up somehow in this rumrunning business and doesn't
want us to know."

"Oh, no!" I cried. "He'd never do a thing like that. He
wouldn't break the law." I could see him on *Irene*'s deck telling
us his ambitions. "He is going to do something outstanding
and splendid to make up to his parents for all the years they
were foreigners here and couldn't talk to anyone. He is going
to prove that even though he is foreign and has a funny name
he can be a better American than any of us."

Aunt Edith smiled. "That sounds just like him. He is so
excitable and always on the defensive."

"Besides," I pressed on, "the night I heard the rumrunners
in the cove Bron was aground on Gull Ledges, so he couldn't
have had anything to do with them. Chester knows he isn't
a rumrunner. If he were, Chester wouldn't talk the way he

does in front of him. He'd arrest him. Chester isn't dumb."

Aunt Edith laughed. "You have convinced me that Bron isn't running rum. I didn't really believe he was. He is too intelligent to take such risks for a little money."

Talk as we might, we couldn't think up an acceptable explanation for Bron's continued absence.

One night a week or so later, I said in despair, "Since Bron left, nothing is any fun. Why don't we find him and ask him why he stays away? Maybe he'll tell us, and maybe we can persuade him to come back again."

Aunt Edith laid her square of patchwork in her lap. "No. I'll never force myself on Bron."

"But, Aunt Edith," I'm afraid I whined — tears were gathering in my eyes — "we all miss him, not just you and me, but everyone. Can't we find him and just ask him? It won't do any harm."

Aunt Edith, who usually avoided caresses, reached out and with a gentleness that reminded me of my mother, patted my knee before she spoke. "I can't, but I guess you can. If you are very unhappy, perhaps you should." She gave me a long, anxious look before she picked up her sewing and went on in her usual crisp, matter-of-fact manner. "No one can make Bron come back or tell us his reasons for staying away. He is free to do as he pleases and he's answerable to no one, except his own conscience. We have no claim on him. But if you want to find him and ask him why he stays away, well, go ahead."

Before I went to sleep that night I had determined that the very next day I would seek out Bron and ask him why he was avoiding us. Nothing, it seemed to me, that he might tell me could be worse than dragging along without him. I would tell him how much we all missed him, how Aunt Edith and I

talked about him almost every night, and worried about him
too. Surely he would explain everything, come back, and we
would all be happy again.

Perfidy

SINCE THE NEXT MORNING WAS FINE I decided to go after Bron
in the catboat. I was most likely to find him at either the town
wharf or the yacht club, a long, tiresome walk but a pleasant
sail. I hoped Freddy would come with me. He always had
a softening influence on hard hearts. Freddy, however, had
agreed to look over old barns and garages with Chester, who
was considering buying one or the other and moving it next to
his own garage for an annex. Chester picked Freddy up at
seven-thirty when he delivered his mother at Cousin Harriet's.
I got out of the house as soon after breakfast as I could and,
with my sail bag over my shoulder, was just leaving our driveway when I was hailed from behind.

"Hey! Wait up!"

I looked back to see Mary beating her way across the field,
tacking clumsily around the beach-plum bushes. She ran knock-
kneed in her high heels, the way ladies do. She drew up pant-
ing with her bracelets clanking.

"What's eating on the 'It Girl'?" I asked pleasantly.

"Lay off the kidding, Jerry. I can't take it. Not today."

"What's the matter?"

"Everything. I'm all cut up. I'm a nervous wreck." She
clutched her throat and screwed up her eyes to show how much
she suffered.

"Disappointed in love?" I asked.

Mary groaned. "It's easy for you who've never been in love to kid about it, and he talks to you, he smiles at you, he asks you onto his boat." Mary gave me a baleful look. "I never thought the day would come that I'd be envious of you, Jerusha Faunce, but I'd give anything to be to him what you are. It's not much, but it's better than being spurned, which is what I am."

"Are you, by any chance, talking about Bron?"

"Who else?"

"Where do you see him these days?" I asked with a cunning I hadn't realized I possessed.

"At the yacht club mostly. Sometimes I row out with a message when he's in *Irene* on the mooring."

"Do you see much of him?"

"I see him. My knees go weak. I shake all over. My heart does somersaults in my breast." Mary screwed up her eyes again and whacked her chest.

"And what does he do?"

"I already told you. He spurns me. You don't have to rub it in."

"I didn't mean to," I said.

"For the past two weeks, Jerry, I've been so miserable. You've no idea."

"Yes, I have. I've been miserable, too."

As usual Mary was too taken up with her own feelings to pay attention to mine. She went right ahead as if I hadn't said anything.

"I suffer most over Bron, but there's The Hag, too. At the dance after the bazaar you wouldn't believe what she did. She marched right out on the dance floor and dragged me off by

the hair. Actually. I mean by the hair, all because I was showing some boys how to Charleston. I was never so humiliated in
my life, and I'll never live it down. The kids at the yacht club
all giggle and wink at each other when they see me coming.
I wouldn't go there anymore if it weren't for getting a chance,
now and then, at Bron. Mrs. Munson has changed, too. She is
inconsiderate. She doesn't listen when I tell her about my troubles with Bron and The Hag. She is always busy. This morning she said she had to introduce Dagmar into some new
territory, and she drove off early without even offering to take
me along. She could at least have driven me as far as the yacht
club, but she never thinks of me anymore — just herself. I'd
have had to walk all the way if I hadn't seen you starting off
with your sail bag. Now you can sail me over to the yacht club,
and I won't have to walk."

"What makes you think I'm sailing to the yacht club?"

"Why not? You might as well sail there as anywhere, and
after all, it's the least you can do for an old friend in need."

Mary's colossal insolence floored me. I could think of no
reason for not taking her. I couldn't even think of a stinging
retort.

Out in the bay the wind was fresh, and the water was choppy.
I made Mary sit forward, and I took considerable satisfaction
in watching the spray break over her. I also enjoyed coming
about without warning her and then yelling angrily because she
got her head in the way of the boom. We were still two long
tacks away from the yacht club when I spotted *Irene*. She
wasn't on her mooring. She was bobbing up and down and
straining on her sea anchor, well out in the bay. I'd have
noticed her sooner if I hadn't been so busy making Mary uncomfortable. It seemed clear to me that *Irene* was having

engine trouble, and it was my duty to sail over and offer to help. What a lucky opening this was! First I'd offer help, then I'd work around to my real business with Bron. I planned how I would slip neatly under *Irene*'s lee side and, without so much as a bump, lower my sail and tie onto her stern. Absorbed in my sailing, I forgot about Mary until, this time by accident, the boom konked her on the head and very nearly knocked her overboard.

"Squat down in the bottom," I shouted, "and keep down until I've tied up."

I came alongside *Irene* just as I had planned, made fast to a ring in her stern and lowered the sail.

Bron wasn't bent over the motor in the cockpit as I'd expected to find him. I climbed over *Irene*'s stern.

"Bron," I called, not very loud, for I felt uneasy about coming aboard without being asked. No one answered. I went forward and called again, a little louder. Bron opened the cabin door, closed it behind him, bounded up into the cockpit and halted abruptly a few steps in front of me.

"What's the matter? Is something wrong at home, I mean at The Haven? Why did you come here?" His eyes glanced over me and around over the water in a worried sort of way.

"Nothing's the matter. I thought you had engine trouble. I sailed over to see if I could help."

Bron didn't smile as if he were relieved that we were all well at The Haven or glad I'd come to help. "Nothing's the matter with the engine," he said. "I don't need any help. Thank you just the same."

I gathered my courage. "I — we — wondered why you hadn't been to see us for so long."

"Oh." Bron looked down at his feet and pulled at his chin.

"Of course, quite natural. You see, I'm very busy. I haven't had any time." He threw back his head and seemed to be addressing himself to the catboat's mast more than to me. "I'm writing a paper, a very difficult paper. It's due before I start back to school. I've put it off much too long. I've got to finish it. As a matter of fact, I anchored out here so I could work without being disturbed." Bron continued not to look at me. His face, usually so mobile, had taken on a wooden look, and he rocked stiffly back and forth on the balls of his feet, like a rocking horse.

"I — we —" I began again.

"Of all the . . ." exclaimed Bron, and clamped his teeth together so hard that I heard the click. His eyes narrowed. He glared past me at the catboat. "So!" And he clamped his mouth shut again.

I glanced over my shoulder and saw Mary's head duck down behind *Irene*'s stern.

"Jerry," said Bron, "you must sail away this minute." He spoke quietly, but his eyes were so hard and angry as he looked straight into mine that I fell back, frightened.

"Please, Bron, I didn't want . . ."

"No, I'm sure you didn't," Bron interrupted me. "It doesn't make any difference. You sail away now, quick, and don't ever come aboard again without being asked. Do you understand?"

I nodded, scrambled onto *Irene*'s stern deck, and tried to untie the catboat's bowline, but tears started into my eyes so I couldn't see the knot. Bron took it from me, untied it, and pulled the catboat in so I could climb aboard. "I'm sorry, Jerry," he said, "but you must leave me alone. I mean it."

He threw the catboat's line to me and stood watching until, ever so clumsily, I hoisted the sail and got the catboat around into the wind and on a tack. I was too hurt and astonished to care very much about where I was sailing or how, and tears kept welling into my eyes so I couldn't see where I was going anyway.

"If you don't watch out," said Mary, "you'll go on Gull Ledges." I wiped my eyes and tried to see where I was. "Never mind taking me to the yacht club now," Mary went on. "Just take me back to the cove. It's that way" — she pointed — "and don't talk to me. I've got a lot of food for thought."

I had changed my course before the outrageousness of Mary hit me and filled me with a fury that, for once, I was able to express.

"I'll take you back to the cove because that's where I want to go myself," I shouted. "I'm not your chauffeur, and I didn't ask you to come with me, and you're the one who does all the talking. Nothing would make me happier than not to have to listen to you for a change. You needn't worry about *me* interrupting *you*. The longer you keep your mouth shut the happier I am."

The outburst eased my feelings and even seemed to make a small dent in Mary.

"Okay," she said. "Okay, but watch what you're doing. You know I can't swim very well, and I'm too young to die."

We exchanged no more words until we had tied up in the cove and I was rowing us in in the skiff.

"It's all clear now," said Mary, "and I was a dumbbell not to catch on before."

I was in no mood to humor her by asking what she was talking about. I rowed on in silence.

"We butted in on a rendezvous, Jerry. That's what we did. They're having an affair."

"Dry up," I said, "and get out and help me pull up the skiff."

Mary got out and made gestures as if she was helping, but she wasn't really, and all the time she had a know-it-all smile on her face. She made me sick. I tied up the skiff, picked up my sail bag, and started for home. Mary came right after me.

"Your wonderful Bron and Mrs. Munson are having an affair. It's been going on all summer. Boy, was I dumb not to catch on sooner, but a lot of other people are dumber than me, like Mr. Munson, and The Hag — and you, Jerry, and your snooty Aunt Edith who think no one has a right to Bron but yourselves."

"You're crazy," I said. "You've been thinking too hard, and it's injured your brain."

"Not me," said Mary. "Bron and Mrs. Munson are having an illicit, clandestine love affair, and *Irene*'s cabin is their love nest. It's just like the movies. Wow!"

"Why don't you stop making up lies and mind your own business and shut up?"

"I'm not making anything up. Mrs. Munson was in *Irene*'s cabin when we were there just now."

"You are so making it up. The cabin door was closed. You couldn't see inside."

"You must need glasses, Jerry" — Mary smiled at me in such a patronizing way it was all I could do not to punch her — "or you'd have seen Mrs. Munson's hat and her big white bag with 'Dagmar' written on it lying right out in plain sight on the bench in the cockpit."

I recalled that something white had been lying on a bench, but I had been so wrapped up in my own business with Bron that I hadn't noticed what it was.

"Maybe she forgot them."

Mary shook her head. "Mrs. Munson never forgets her bag. It's got everything she needs in it."

"They were probably having a business discussion."

"Don't act dumber than you are already," said Mary. "The evidence, as they say in the movies, all points to an assignation between Mrs. M. and Mr. Z. in the cabin of the *Irene* this morning."

"A what?" The word sounded sinister to me.

"Assignation — spelled a-s-s-i-g-n-a-t-i-o-n. It means a meeting between lovers, and they weren't just pitching woo."

"They can't be lovers," I retorted. "Mrs. Munson is married already. So there, smarty."

"Honestly, Jerry, 'Naive' should be your middle name."

Here was another word I didn't know. I could only glare at Mary and snarl, "It should not."

"N-a-i-v-e, pronounced nigh-eve. It means wholesome and sort of dim." Mary smiled patiently.

"And your middle name should be 'Liar,' spelled l-i-a-r, pronounced *liar*," I shouted.

"Keep your shirt on," said Mary, "and listen. You might learn something. If Mrs. Munson was really just handing samples of antisunburn cream over to Bron, or if she was really just telling him about a group she'd got up to go fishing with him, why did she tell me she was taking Dagmar into new territory this morning, and why didn't she give me a lift to the yacht club, since she was going right there herself? Why did Bron anchor *Irene* out in the middle of the bay if he was just having a business discussion with Mrs. Munson, and why did they have it inside *Irene*'s cabin with the door shut on a nice sunny day like this? Why did Bron act so embarrassed when you came aboard? Why didn't he tell you he was having a business discussion with Mrs. Munson, instead of making up all that stuff about writing a paper? Why did he get so mad when he saw me? Why was he in such a rush to get rid of us both?" Mary paused to give me time to take this all in. "You'll have to admit it, Jerry. Something is very fishy."

I couldn't refute either Mary's facts or her insinuations, but I didn't want to talk to her. I started walking faster. Mary trotted right after me.

"Are you going to tell your Aunt Edith?"

"Leave me alone," I muttered.

"I'm going to tell The Hag" — Mary smacked her lips — "because it will make her so mad and look so silly after she took such a shine to Mrs. Munson. I'm going to open the next letter Mrs. Munson gives me to deliver to Bron and read it and then show it to The Hag. It'll be a love letter, making another assignation. Believe you me, Jerry, that's what it will be. With written evidence like that right under her nose, The Hag can't say I made it all up." I walked faster still. Mary panted along right at my elbow. "What a stink there'll be when Uncle Edward hears that The Hag, herself, hand-picked a Fallen Woman to be my chaperone. Zowie! It's better than the movies." She gave a whoop of laughter and breathed hard.

I couldn't stand her a minute longer. I broke into a run and ran all the rest of the way home.

Aunt Edith was on a stepladder washing the kitchen walls. I couldn't talk to her. I went up to my room and tried to think up reasons why Mary was wrong, but as I thought of Bron and remembered the things he'd done during the summer that had seemed unlike him, I had to admit that Mary's theory explained an awful lot.

Right at the beginning of the summer, Grandpa had complained that Bron didn't come to The Haven as often as he used to. He hadn't come for supper to welcome Freddy and me the night we arrived, or for breakfast the next morning either, though Aunt Edith had been expecting him. He hadn't had any definite excuse. He had just said he was busy. The night of the fog and the dance he had had an excuse. He said he was stuck on Gull Ledges. I'd thought it wasn't like him to run *Irene* on a reef, even in a bad fog. He knew the harbor too well, and he was very careful of *Irene*. I remembered how Chester had said he had thought Bron was a better seaman than to do a stupid thing like that. That night Mrs. Munson had left the church while I was serving supper, before the dance began. I remembered how she had stopped me on her way out and spoken to me.

Horrified at the way the evidence against Bron was piling up, I summoned to mind those happy, sunny afternoons on *Irene* when he and Freddy and I swam and talked and drank sarsaparilla, and Bron always came home with us for supper and stayed late into the evening. He wasn't having any — whatever it was Mary had called it — love affair with Mrs. Munson then. He was his old self, gay and open, loving us all and happy to be with us. Suddenly I saw Mary dripping and shivering in the cockpit of *Irene* on the afternoon she had swum out. I saw Bron ordering her off the boat and back to shore. How angry he had been, how unlike his usual self, and all because Mary hadn't brought him the message from Mrs. Munson that he expected.

My heart sank. The harder I tried to disqualify Mary's vile theory, the better it seemed to fit. If I accepted it, my Bron, the one I loved, ceased to exist. He was just a disguise assumed by the real, false Bron. I couldn't give up Bron so easily. I told myself that Mary had distorted everything in her nasty way. Mary was poison. There must be a better explanation for Bron's strange behavior which left him honest and true as he had always been. I dragged through the long afternoon waiting for evening and a chance to share my story and my trouble with Aunt Edith. She was grown-up and clever. No one could call her whatever it was Mary had called me. Surely she could demolish Mary's theory with new facts or with new and brilliant interpretations of the old ones. If she couldn't bring Bron back to us bodily, at least she could restore him to his true self. I counted on her.

When Dr. Davis arrived while we were reading after dinner and announced his intention of spending the evening with Aunt Edith, I vowed to sit up in the parlor with them until he left (and I hoped my presence would cause him to leave earlier than usual) so I could talk to Aunt Edith. Fortunately, he was called away on an emergency soon after he arrived. Aunt Edith came back into the parlor after seeing him off and seeing Grandpa and Freddy to bed.

Despair

I COULD TELL BY YOUR EXPRESSION, Jerusha," she said, "that you have something to say to me. Did you find Bron? Did he tell you why he has stayed away so long?" She sat down with her sewing in her lap, leaning toward me, eager to hear what I had to tell. I told the whole story and waited to hear her reaction to it. While I was talking she had bent her head over her sewing, though she hadn't taken a stitch. After I had finished she stayed bent over and silent for so long that I began to think she had forgotten I was there.

"What do you think?" I ventured. "You don't think Mary's right?"

Aunt Edith lifted her hands to cover her face and went on sitting, bent over, with her face covered for another long time. Finally she let her hands fall to her sides, stood up, and began walking very quickly up and down the parlor. Her sewing fell out of her lap to the floor and she stepped on it without noticing. I picked it up for her, and she didn't notice that either. When she passed near the lamp I could see her face, but it seemed to have no expression at all.

"I don't want to believe it," I ventured again, "but it fits so many things."

"Yes, yes," said Aunt Edith, more to herself than to me.

For some minutes she walked, and I sat, and neither of us said anything. I wanted so much to have Aunt Edith reassure me. I prodded her.

"I thought you could think of reasons why Mary is wrong." Aunt Edith shook her head and went on walking. "He wouldn't do what Mary says he's been doing and all the time lie to us and pretend he was the way he's always been, would he?"

Aunt Edith finally stopped walking. "It's so unlike him, so unlike what I've always believed about him." She dropped into a chair and slumped there hugging her arms as if she were cold. She turned to me. "I'd give anything not to believe what you've told me, but it all fits. It fits so terribly well."

"You mean you believe, you really believe that Bron and Mrs. Munson . . . ?" I couldn't go on.

"I haven't any choice," said Aunt Edith in a flat, weary voice.

"What can we do?" I begged her.

Slowly Aunt Edith straightened her back. She lifted her chin in her old, proud way. "The best thing we can do is forget about Bron and turn our attention to — to worthier objects."

"I can't forget about him," I said. (I'm afraid I whined.) "I love him too much."

Aunt Edith stood up and lifted her chin a little higher. "You must try. It's happened before that girls have loved young men who didn't love them and they have got over it. It happens all the time. You can forget him, if you just try. You're young, other things will turn up to interest you. It's hard for you now, but you'll soon feel better."

I didn't believe her. I was sure that I could never get over Bron. "Shouldn't we do something to make him come back to us?" I asked. "We can't just let him run off with a — with a — Fallen Woman. After all, he's one of our family."

"Not any longer," said Aunt Edith. "Not after this." She began to walk again.

"We can't just abandon him."

"No," replied Aunt Edith, "he has already abandoned us."

"Maybe, if we give him a chance, he could explain." I was whining again.

"Explain!" Aunt Edith stopped in front of me. "He could explain all right, with more lies. He lies so easily and so well." She tossed her head. Her beautiful eyes glistened strangely in the lamplight. "I'm tired of his lies, and of him, too. He can find a home somewhere else." She turned her head away. "Please, Jerusha," she said in a sort of whisper, "will you turn out the lights and look in on Freddy. I'm upset. I — I'm going right to bed." She almost ran out of the parlor and I thought, though I wasn't sure, that I heard her sob.

I did as she asked me and went to bed with a heavy heart.

I woke next morning to gray twilight. Tendrils of fog twined among the tendrils of wisteria outside my window. When I got up and looked out I could barely make out the shape of the arborvitae jungle, and the top half of the flagpole was obliterated. The weather was as miserable as I. In the kitchen, Aunt Edith had turned on the electric light and was giving breakfast as usual to Grandpa, Freddy, and Sunbeam. She looked pale in the yellow glare of the electricity. Grandfather and Freddy didn't notice that her cheery remarks were strained, or that her smile was stiff, but I did. When the two of them had been seen off (by this time Freddy was leaving every morning with Chester as regularly as a working man), Aunt Edith told me not to tell what we knew about Bron. When Grandpa or Freddy asked about him, we must put them off as best we could. The truth would be too great a shock for Grandpa, and Freddy wouldn't understand. I guess I'd still had some small hope that during the night Aunt Edith would think up some way to clear Bron. Her assumption that he was as guilty as Mary had made him out killed that hope.

Aunt Edith said she was done with the cleaning and would devote the day to preparation for her classes. She would work in Grandpa's study where it was quiet, and since the weather was so dismal, I might build a fire in the parlor and read there. I would be more comfortable than up in my room. She lent me all her current detective stories. Between the fire, which took a lot of poking, and the books, I got through the morning and half the afternoon. Then an unexpected diversion arrived in the form of a visit from Mary.

"I've done it," she said.

"Done what?"

"I've not delivered the message, and was I ever right! Here, get a load of this." Mary thrust an envelope under my nose. It was addressed in a scrawl to Mr. Zebra.

I took the sheet of notepaper out of the envelope, unfolded it, and read. "B.Z. General alert. Tonight's date and all future dates off until I let you know. No time for details. Wait. Trust me. D.M."

"It doesn't sound very loving to me." I handed back the note.

"That's because she wrote it in such a hurry, and I was watching her," said Mary. "I went over after lunch because she was going to take me to Houghton Landing to see *Fallen Blossoms*. It's a rerun, and I've seen it before, but it's swell. Mrs. Munson had a suitcase by the door, and she had her hat on, and she was running around stuffing things into her handbag. She'd forgotten all about me and the movie. When I reminded her she said she was terribly sorry but she was called away on urgent business and couldn't take me after all. She looked at me for a minute and smiled sweetly — only now my eyes were opened, and I knew that that sweet smile was false, false, false!" Mary smacked her forehead with her hand and shuddered, then went on in a simpering imitation of Mrs. Munson. " 'Will you be a lamb, Mary, and get this note out to Mr. Zebra. He's sure to be in his boat, moored off the town wharf. I'll drive you down and drop you there. I'm really terribly sorry about *Fallen Blossoms,* but this is an emergency. Mr. Munson just telephoned and I must fly.' "

Mary gave a snort of disgust and changed back to her own voice. "Of course I said I was dying to take her note to Mr. Zebra, so she dashed it off and sealed it, and here it is. She drove down to the wharf so fast through the fog that I was scared silly. I was so glad to get out of that car alive that I didn't mind walking home one bit. Besides, it gave me time to read the note and think. I decided I couldn't stand to miss *Fallen Blossoms* — it's a real classic — and that I'd call up Ken, long distance, and ask him to come down and take me to the evening show. I'd offer to pay for his gas and his ticket, too. When I was still mad for Bron I didn't care if I never saw Ken again, but I kept writing to him and stringing him along, just in case. I telephoned him from the Munsons' cottage. She'd forgotten to lock the door. I never make long-distance calls on The Hag's telephone because when the bill comes in at the end of the month she checks over all the calls and has to know who made which one and why before she'll pay the bill. I hope I never get stingy with my money like her." Mary sighed. "I got Ken all right, and he's still crazy about me. He said he'd do anything to see his poor little rich girl again. He's going to drive down in the delivery truck as soon as he gets through work. He'll be here in plenty of time to make the eight-thirty show."

"If he doesn't get lost in the fog."

"He won't. He's too crazy to see me, and anyway I'm meeting him down where Station Avenue crosses Haskell. He won't have to find his way up here. I'm not taking any chances of The Hag's seeing him. She'd be sure to spoil everything." Mary considered the note she was holding, then replaced it carefully in its envelope. "I'm not sure when I'll show this to The Hag. I might do it when she's telling her bridge club about how clever she was to get Mrs. Munson to chaperone me around, and what a fine, worthy person Mrs. Munson is, and what a good influence on me. I might say, casually, to the old biddies, 'I've just found out that Mrs. Munson is having an illicit, clandestine love affair with Bron Zebra. I thought you should know.' Or maybe I won't do it that way at all. What do you think, Jerry?"

I shrugged.

"You're awfully quiet today," said Mary. "What's happened to the dazzling repartee and the snappy comebacks?"

I shrugged again.

"I suppose you're feeling pretty blue about losing Bron. I know how it is. I've been through it myself. If I'd thought of it in time, I'd have asked Ken to bring a friend for you. We could have double-dated. *Fallen Blossoms* would cheer you up, if anything would."

This was the only time in the whole summer that Mary had shown any interest in me other than as a sounding board for herself. In my forlorn state, I was grateful for her thoughtfulness.

"Thanks," I said. "Thanks a lot."

"I must dash," exclaimed Mary, "and try to do something with my hair. The fog has taken out every bit of wave. Keep your chin up. There's a silver lining somewhere. Ta-ta." She clanked her bracelets at me and left. I never saw her again. Though Cousin Harriet continued to summer in Sewell right up to the beginning of the Second World War, Mary never came again. She was either in boarding school in Switzerland, or traveling with a chaperone in Europe, or, later, living in Hollywood.

Bloodshed

A T FIVE, when Chester brought Freddy home, it was dark as night. Chester came in to be sure that Grandpa and the Electric had got safely home, as they had, and to advise us to stay indoors for the rest of the evening.

"We'll be patrolling," he told Aunt Edith, "and with the fog and all, there may be trouble. It might be a good idea for the Reverend to sleep with his windows shut and to take a sleeping pill."

We were in the parlor after supper, reading, when we saw two yellow blobs nose up the drive. A minute later, Dr. Davis came in, looking pleased. Fog was nothing to him. When he'd made up his mind to do something, he did it. After seeing his last patient, he had sneaked away without leaving a telephone number where he could be reached. He wasn't going to be cheated out of another evening with us. By "us" we all knew he meant Aunt Edith. He escorted Grandpa to bed and persuaded him to take the sleeping pill. I knew I didn't stand a chance of talking to Aunt Edith alone. I went to bed when Freddy did and read myself to sleep.

I woke suddenly and sat up, aware that some sound, sharp and strange, had roused me. A piercing yell, with something familiar about its timbre, split the night and was abruptly stifled. A hubbub of pounding feet and shouting followed. I ran to my window and looked into a black curtain of fog. Below me, our porch light went on, throwing a dim beam into the blackness. The screen door opened and banged shut. I saw Grandpa, clad in his nightshirt and carrying a lantern, march out and disappear into the fog.

"Is anyone hurt?" Grandpa's beautiful voice rose like organ music above the hubbub.

"Yes, a man's been shot," a voice shouted back.

"Bring him here," called Grandpa. "This way. There's a doctor here." Ever so faintly I could see streaks of light wavering through the fog as, I guessed, Grandpa lifted up his lantern and swung it.

The voices grew louder and clearer. There were exclamations and grunts. "Where's he hit?" "I don't know." "Where are we taking him? I'm all turned around." "Over where the lantern is waving." "I hope it's not far. He's bleeding all over me." Grandpa's voice rose again. "This way, this way." There were more grunts and some curses. I recognized Chester's voice. "For God's sake, hurry, or he'll bleed to death." Grandpa and his lantern, followed by six men carrying the wounded man, materialized out of the fog.

"Right in here," said Grandpa. "Turn right into the kitchen. Lay him on the table. I'll call the doctor." All the figures disappeared under the wisteria. "Doctor Davis, Edith, Jerusha, Freddy!" Grandpa called from inside now. "Bron is here. He's wounded. He's bleeding. Come at once."

I ran out of my room and down the stairs. Freddy bounded out of his door. We both stopped at the foot of the stairs, horrified to see a trail of blood across the floor and blood spattered on the walls. Chester came out the kitchen door with Aunt Edith limp in his arms. He carried her across the hall to the parlor. Dr. Davis came out of the kitchen. He was in his shirt sleeves and spattered with blood. He saw us on the stairs.

"Get sheets," he said, "quick."

I bolted upstairs to the linen closet, grabbed a pile of sheets, and carried them into the kitchen. Dr. Davis and Grandpa were bent over Bron on the kitchen table. There was blood on the floor. Dr. Davis turned to me, grabbed a sheet, and began ripping it in strips. "Watch me," he said as he ripped. "Do the others the same way, and hand them to your grandfather to

fold." I ripped, and Grandpa folded, and Dr. Davis pressed the wads of sheet on top of the other onto the spurting wound in Bron's thigh.

"Jerusha, you rip and fold now. Mr. Faunce, you keep the pressure on the wound while I put on a tourniquet." With one of my torn strips and a wooden spoon, Dr. Davis made a tourniquet and tied it around Bron's thigh just above the wound. He tightened and loosened it at intervals. I went on ripping and folding. Grandpa pressed new wads of sheeting on the wound as the old ones became soaked with blood. Gradually the bleeding slackened.

"Jerusha," said Dr. Davis without looking up, "get all the dinner plates and put them in the oven to heat. Put on a kettle of water to heat. Get blankets and bring them here. If you know where there's a hot water bottle, bring it. Be quick."

First I put the plates in the oven, then I brought the blankets and went upstairs again to find the hot water bottle. When I came down with it, Bron's body was covered with blankets and Dr. Davis was putting away a hypodermic needle. The tea kettle had been on the back of the stove, so the water was hot. I filled the hot water bottle. Dr. Davis placed it at Bron's feet. I brought the hot plates from the oven and Dr. Davis slipped them under the blankets against Bron's body. He felt Bron's pulse.

"I think he's going to be all right."

For the first time since I'd started work I had a moment to look into Bron's face. It was ash white, and his beautiful, golden hair lay in damp, grayish wads around his forehead. His eyelids flickered. His gray lips moved, and he muttered something unintelligible.

"He'll be coming around soon," said Dr. Davis. He smiled

at me. "You're a great little nurse. A lot of R.N.'s can't keep their heads and follow orders when a patient is bleeding the way he was. Poor Edy keeled right over, and Chester and those policemen of his turned green and cleared out. They were no good at all, but you, Jerry, and you, Reverend, acted as if you'd worked in operating rooms all your lives. How do you account for it?"

"In my case it is quite simple," replied Grandpa. "As a clergyman I am often called to sit with the sick and dying. As a young man, during the war with Spain, I served as a chaplain and spent a good deal of time in the hospitals, where the conditions were truly shocking." He drew up a chair beside the table and, reaching under the blankets, took one of Bron's hands in both his own. "When he comes to," continued Grandpa, "he will be reassured to feel the warmth of another hand holding his. I often held the hands of those poor soldiers, and I think it helped them. The doctors could do very little for them. There were no bandages, no medicines, sometimes not even water." Grandpa lifted his gentle eyes to us and shook his beautiful white head. In his spattered nightshirt he was an awe-inspiring sight. Dr. Davis blinked.

"As for little Jerusha," Grandpa went on, "she is, as you know, subject to nosebleeds when she is under stress. I believe she is having one now." And so I was, but I hadn't noticed. From somewhere, Grandpa produced a clean piece of sheet and handed it to me. "Press that to your nose, little Jerusha, and tilt your head back. It will soon stop. These nosebleeds have, no doubt, accustomed little Jerusha to the sight of blood and also, she takes after my late, dear wife who was up to anything. She and I will nurse Bron here at The Haven. I will not permit another member of my family to be taken away to that hospital.

Little Jerusha, put a fresh cloth to your nose. Doctor, will you fetch some more plates? These are getting cold."

We both did as Grandpa told us. While Dr. Davis handed Grandpa the plates, one by one, he stared at him as if he had never seen him before. A few minutes later, he reasserted himself by explaining in his most official manner that, in a case like this where danger of infection was slight, home nursing was exactly what he would recommend. Bron must be kept warm and absolutely quiet until he had regained some strength. After that, for at least a month, he should stay in bed and move as little as possible. The bullet, which had gone right through his thigh and severed an artery, had also severed nerves and ligaments. They should be allowed plenty of time to heal and then be exercised gradually back to use. Patience was to be our motto if we wanted Bron to walk normally again.

"We will follow your instructions, Doctor," said Grandpa. "And now, will you see about cleaning up the kitchen? Perhaps some of the men will help. Little Jerusha, if your nosebleed is better, perhaps you should tell Edith that Bron will get well. I'm sure she is very anxious." He bent over Bron and stroked his forehead.

"I never guessed the old gentleman had so much spunk in him," whispered Dr. Davis.

"I am a mild man," said Grandpa, who had overheard him, "but I can be firm. Now, Doctor, I insist that you do not give me any more of those sleeping pills. After you left me last night I was able to open the windows in my bedroom and let in some fresh air, but I had no way of regurgitating your sleeping pill. Consequently, I didn't sleep a wink. When I heard strange noises outside I got up to investigate. I was in the shed lighting my lantern when I heard two shots, one of which hit our poor

Bron. I heard a scream too, a female scream — we must inquire after Harriet and little Mary in the morning. Of course I went out at once with my lantern to offer help in case someone had been hurt, and, as it turned out, it was lucky I did. However, in general, Doctor, I prefer to sleep at night, and your pills make sleep impossible." Bron groaned and stirred. Grandpa bent close to his face and muttered words I couldn't hear. Dr. Davis and I hastened to carry out his instructions.

Aunt Edith and Freddy (who had been frightened by the blood in the hall and fled to Chester in the parlor) were put to bed. Chester ordered some of the stronger policemen to clean up the hall and kitchen and carry Bron upstairs to my bedroom. We agreed that this was the best room for Bron because it was close to the bathroom and the stairs to the kitchen. I made up a cot for myself in Freddy's room. Dr. Davis left, and Grandpa sat with Bron for the rest of the night.

Edith's Narrative

Aftermath

EARLY NEXT MORNING, before anyone else was up, Chester limped into the kitchen where I was getting breakfast. He had just delivered Cousin Harriet and Mary to the 7:02 and brought his mother back to close the two Cornish cottages for the season. Hubbub at midnight — shots, screams, a man wounded, and, worst of all, her own granddaughter out with a boy in a delivery truck — all this, plus the discovery that her esteemed tenants were bootleggers who kept a stock of choice Canadian whiskey along with the latest in unlicensed radio equipment in Cousin Harriet's own garage — all this had broken the old lady's nerve. Although it was only the end of July and the worst of the heat was yet to come, she had fled with Mary to New York. Chester had advised the flight. The newspapers, he said, could be counted on to make the most of the story. All the rest of the summer we might expect sightseers gaping at the Cornish cottages and garages and rummaging around for bottles of whiskey that the Internal Revenue men might have overlooked when they trucked the contraband away. Chester had already ordered guards to be posted around The Haven to keep off the first rush of sightseers so Bron would have the quiet he needed to get well.

I didn't know exactly what had happened to bring about the violence of the night before, and I was more confused than anything by what Chester was telling me. Chester, however, was in no hurry to make things clear to me. He sat down at the kitchen table and allowed, with many a headshake and sigh, that at one time he had suspected Bron of being mixed up in the Munsons' bootlegging activities. *Irene,* with her black paint and her new equipment, was such a handy boat for the work, and Bron, with his knowledge of the harbor, could slip in and out under the very noses of the Coast Guard and not be caught. Bron had been seeing a lot of Mrs. Munson over the summer, too. Chester knew all about their business arrangements and meetings. Chester said he owed Bron two apologies: one for suspecting him of being a rumrunner, and the other for letting him get shot. I said nothing about what I knew about Bron and Mrs. Munson. I sat straight and still and waited politely while Chester hummed and sighed and shook his head some more. The weariness and depression I felt must have shown in my face, because Chester gave me a long, commiserating look, then took my hand, patted it, smiled, and told me to cheer up because there was a silver lining to the whole mess after all. Bron had had a bullet through his leg — true — and the Munsons had got clean away, but after what happened last night Bron couldn't possibly be convicted of rumrunning. There was no evidence against him. Absolutely none. We must be grateful for that.

In an effort to seem more like my everyday self, I said that I would be even more grateful if Chester would explain just what had happened so I would know what he was talking about. Chester winced and muttered that Bron meant a lot to him, and he couldn't forget what a close call Bron had had, and that he (Chester) thought I cared a lot about Bron too and would want to know, before anything, that Bron was all square with the law and had nothing to worry about.

I knew Chester was shocked by my brusqueness. Yet, if I hadn't hidden my feelings with a matter-of-fact, everyday manner — if, then or later, I had once given in, I'd have gone all to pieces and cried like any silly half-baked girl. I couldn't afford to pamper myself with hysterics or a nervous break-down. I was responsible for Father, the children, The Haven, and a new job in September, and I was afraid to let myself go in any way for fear that I could not pull myself back. How stupid to digress in this way. I set out to record — not my feelings, but the events, as Chester told them to me, that led up to the violence of that July night in 1926. I shall now do so. I remember them all very well.

Chester Explains

CHESTER REMINDED ME that earlier in the summer, with Freddy's help, he had strung a radio antenna from the lightning rod on top of our cupola to the lightning rod on the gable of our shed. He said it had greatly improved the reception of Father's radio, though of course Father had never noticed the difference. The antenna, Chester explained, was just an uncovered wire with glass insulators at either end where it was attached to the lightning rods. The leading wire, insulated, dropped from midway on the antenna to the roof and ran down it to a corner under the eaves. It entered the house there along with the electric and telephone wires from the street. Inside the house, Chester had carried his wire along moldings and down through closets to the radio in Father's study. The arrangement of the wires, inside and out, was so unobtrusive that I, for one, had never noticed them. Chester said that you wouldn't notice a radio antenna on a roof unless you were looking for it, or unless the sun happened to strike on it just right or on the insulators. That was part of the story.

One evening, shortly after he had strung our antenna, Chester was sitting in his car outside Cousin Harriet's cottage, waiting to drive his mother home after work. He had turned around at the dead end of the road, blown three toots on the horn, and was casting his eye over the two garages (one for each of Cousin Harriet's cottages) which stood side by side, against a background of trees, at the edge of the road. Chester needed an addition to his own garage and was always looking out for something he could buy cheap and move. The garage that went with the Munsons' cottage was open and empty — obviously in use. Cousin Harriet's garage was shut up tight. As Chester looked it over, his eye was caught by sunlight flashing from a wire which, when he looked again, he saw was strung between the lightning rods on the peaks of the two garage roofs. It could be nothing but a radio antenna. To his surprise, he next spotted not one, but two leading wires dropping from two points on the antenna to the roof of the shut-up garage. Chester climbed out of his car and went to make sure that the two leading wires entered Cousin Harriet's garage along with the electric wire from the street. He also tried the big double front door of the garage and the small back door. Both were locked. The two windows were curtained, on the inside, with green shades, lowered and tacked to the window frame.

Chester climbed back into his car and thought about all this until his mother came out. That Cousin Harriet had not one, but two radios in a garage she didn't use struck Chester as fishy. When he reflected further that the two leading wires might just as well connect with one radio sending set and one receiving set, he smelled more than fish. He smelled a rat. On the way home, he asked his mother about Cousin Harriet's garage and learned that the Munsons had rented it for the summer as a storehouse for the cosmetics they were selling in the Sewell area. Chester wondered why a garage used for storage would be wired to receive and send radio messages. He decided he must have a look inside that garage.

He could have broken a lock or a window, but he didn't want to arouse suspicion. He considered posting a policeman in plain clothes to watch the garage and the Munsons for a day or two, but he gave up the idea. His policemen were not trained for sleuthing and, in matters requiring discretion, not to be absolutely trusted. Chester was certain, even early in the summer, that someone at the Coast Guard station was telling someone in the rumrunning business all Lieutenant Dawson's plans almost as soon as the lieutenant thought them up.

Chester believed his policemen were honest, but they were local boys. They had friends and relatives working at the Coast Guard station and, very likely, some working as rum-runners too. A slip of the tongue, an inadvertent confidence,

and the Munsons, if they were managing the local bootlegging, would get the wind up. Chester had just about decided
that he would have to do his own sleuthing, though because of
his bulk and his official status he was far from inconspicuous,
when the solution to his problem dawned on him, simple and
elegant — a true stroke of genius. His mother would be his
sleuth. She was discreet, trustworthy, small and agile enough
to sneak about unseen, and, best of all, above suspicion and
on the spot. Mrs. Bates had neither qualms nor scruples. She
would have done anything for Chester. She set right to work.

She discovered that Mr. Munson drove away early every
morning in one of the Munsons' two cars and was usually not
back until after she (Mrs. Bates) had gone home for the night.
Mrs. Munson, however, visited the closed-up garage almost
every day. She went in by the small back door, locked it behind her, and stayed in the garage for half an hour or so before she came out, locking the door again behind her. Mrs.
Bates never once saw her open the big front garage door, and
she never forgot to lock the back door after she went in or
came out. After two weeks of sleuthing, Mrs. Bates hadn't
got so much as a peep inside. She decided that she must somehow steal Mrs. Munson's keys, unlock the garage, see what was
in it, and return the keys before Mrs. Munson realized they
had been stolen.

Mrs. Munson kept all her keys on a ring in the big, white
bag with "Dagmar" written on it, and she carried the bag
wherever she went. She never left it in her car or on the porch.
Only when she was in the house, with the screen doors latched,
did she put the bag down and, even then, she kept it within
easy reach. When she was in the living room, the bag was on
the telephone table. When she was in the kitchen, the bag was

on a shelf in the pantry. The bag was unguarded only for short intervals when Mrs. Munson ran upstairs to fetch something. Mrs. Bates made these observations on visits to the Munson cottage to borrow or return a cup of sugar, an egg, or later, to help Mrs. Munson with her crocheting. Mrs. Munson, who was always friendly and willing to chat, expressed her admiration of Mrs. Bates's fancy work as displayed at the bazaar. In gratitude, Mrs. Bates offered to teach Mrs. Munson to crochet. This, it turned out, was something Mrs. Munson had wanted to learn ever since she was a little girl back in Indiana. Mrs. Bates lent hooks, thread, and patterns, as well as giving instruction.

Mrs. Munson was upstairs looking for a doily which she was trying to copy on the afternoon that Mrs. Bates, trembling all over, extracted the keys from the bag on the pantry shelf and slipped them in her apron pocket. It took all Mrs. Bates's nerve to control her trembling while she demonstrated a complicated stitch to Mrs. Munson and waited for her to master it. Then, after returning briefly to her own kitchen, Mrs. Bates slipped out through the shrubbery to the back door of Cousin Harriet's garage. When she finally found the right key for the door and opened it, her courage was rewarded with what Chester called an "eyeful." The garage was nearly full of pyramid-shaped parcels wrapped in burlap. Each parcel contained six bottles of Canadian whiskey carefully packed in straw. Empty cartons of various sizes bearing the purple Dagmar label were stacked against a wall, along with a few cartons containing powder, rouge, and sunburn cream. In a corner, barricaded behind the pyramids of whiskey, was a table bearing an instrument panel and earphones. To Mrs. Bates, the apparatus appeared as a confusion of knobs and dials in front

and a tangle of wires behind. She couldn't describe it to Chester as thoroughly as she did the other contents of the garage, but she didn't need to. Chester knew what it was.

Mrs. Bates got out of the garage and back to her own kitchen unobserved. Now she had to return the keys to Mrs. Munson's bag. She had planned how she would do this beforehand. She knocked again on Mrs. Munson's kitchen door, apologized for being such a nuisance, coming back so soon, but wondered if Mrs. Munson had a certain crochet pattern which Mrs. Bates couldn't find among her other patterns and thought she might have lent to Mrs. Munson. While Mrs. Munson was upstairs looking for the nonexistent pattern, Mrs. Bates slipped the keys back into the bag, which, luckily, was still on the pantry shelf.

Chester now had all the evidence he needed to arrest the Munsons, but he wanted to wait, hire a first-class detective to shadow Mr. Munson, and find out who his bosses were. This didn't suit Lieutenant Dawson at all. Though hampered by the absence of the two damaged patrol boats, the lieutenant had recently captured a boat loaded with illegal brandy right in Sewell Harbor. The skipper of the illegal boat had managed to disappear mysteriously while the lieutenant and his crew were tying up their prize at the Coast Guard station; however, the lieutenant was able to turn over the boat and the bottles to the government and was commended for this. Since the damaged patrol boats would soon be back in commission, he was determined to use them to win more glory. Although Chester did not say so, I believe the lieutenant was also jealous of Chester's success. At any rate, he vetoed Chester's suggestion and planned how the Coast Guard, assisted by the local police, would bag the Munsons, along with more rumrunners, boats, liquor, and acclaim in one "grand coup." The French —

Chester assured me — was the lieutenant's, not his own. He pronounced it "coop."

On the first night that there was no moon and the tide was right for the rumrunners to make it in and out of the quiet inlets they favored, the Coast Guard would unleash its repaired patrol boats. Chester's men would guard the inlets to pick up any boats that got past the Coast Guard. More of Chester's men, reinforced with Coast Guard personnel, would surround the Munsons' cottage, arrest them, and seize the garage and its contents.

Chester argued that if, starting with what he knew about the Munsons, he was allowed to work quietly back up the chain of command until he found out who the top executives in the bootlegging business were, then they could be arrested and rumrunning all along the coast would be ended. He said he thought this was a simpler, cheaper, more effective, and less risky plan than the lieutenant's, and he made the lieutenant very angry. The lieutenant dressed him down and told him to obey orders. Chester knew the lieutenant wouldn't hesitate to make trouble for him if he stuck to his guns. He apologized, agreed to obey orders, and only asked that the lieutenant be especially careful to keep his plans secret. The lieutenant told Chester to mind his own business.

Late in the afternoon of the appointed day, Chester posted two of his policemen and two Coast Guard men to watch the Munsons' cottage and the garages. The fog was thick. Both the Munsons' cars were gone, and their cottage was empty. Chester was certain no one saw the guards slip into the shrubbery. Their orders were to keep quiet and out of sight until both the Munsons had come home and were in the cottage. Then one of the policemen was to hoot three times like an owl.

Chester and another policeman, one Bill Acker, would be at the foot of the hill, guarding the cove and waiting for the signal. When they heard it, Bill, who hooted well, would reply with three more hoots. Chester would get the paddy wagon, which was hidden nearby in the bushes, drive up the hill, knock on the Munsons' door, show his warrant, explain to the Munsons that their cottage was surrounded and they could not escape, and, he hoped, arrest them quietly and drive them away.

Chester and Bill waited at the cove. No cars passed bearing the Munsons into the trap, and no hoots from the top of the hill signaled that the Munsons had somehow got past Chester and Bill and were in their cottage. No sounds of a boat nosing up the river or a truck grinding down Haskell Street broke the silence. There was only the darkness and the fog. Midnight passed, and Chester felt in his bones, which by now were aching with weariness and cold, that the Munsons had flown the coop.

He thought of his men, huddled for over six hours now in the Munsons' damp shrubbery. They couldn't even pace up and down to keep warm. If anything happened during the rest of the night, and Chester doubted that anything would, he was sure that he and Bill could handle it. He had just about decided to send the guards at the cottage home to bed, when he heard a motorboat down the river. For ten minutes the sound approached until it stopped about a hundred yards — so Chester reckoned, for he couldn't see anything — offshore. He heard someone moving about, tying up the boat, boarding a skiff, and rowing straight toward the place where he stood. He had known for some time that the motor he heard was *Irene*'s. Sad at heart, he accosted Bron as he grounded the skiff and jumped ashore. Bron seemed more annoyed than anything when Chester informed him that he was being held on suspicion of smuggling, until Bill had searched *Irene* for evidence.

"Not again?" said Bron, and added, nonsensically Chester thought, "Et tu, Chester?"

"I'm sorry," said Chester, "I wish it was anyone except you."

"Don't feel bad," replied Bron. "The Coast Guard has already stopped me and searched me three times and let me go because they couldn't find what they were looking for. Go ahead, search *Irene*. I'll wait. I won't run away."

Bill rowed out, searched *Irene,* and returned to assure Chester there wasn't a bottle to be found on board. Chester was so relieved that he slapped Bron on the back, then shook his hand until Bron begged him to stop because he was hurting him.

"Why do you go out in fog like this?" demanded Chester, annoyed, for all he was relieved, that Bron had worried him so. "Last time you got stuck on Gull Ledges. This time you were lucky not to get yourself shot up. Why can't you stay home like a sensible man?"

"I guess it's my Polish blood," said Bron. "It makes me do crazy things. Will it be all right," he added after a pause, "if I go on up the hill now?"

Chester assumed that Bron planned to go to The Haven. He explained that the Munsons' cottage was under guard, that the men had been there a long time, in the cold and damp, with nothing to do, and by now were likely to shoot at any strange noise they heard, just out of ill temper and boredom. He said he was about to drive up to the Munsons' cottage in the paddy wagon to dismiss the guard and take them home, and Bron could drive up with him. He would sound the siren to be sure the guard knew who was coming. Bron wanted to know why on earth the Munsons' cottage was under guard. Since Chester was certain by now that the Munsons had got clean away, he saw no harm in telling Bron about what he had found in their garage and what he thought of the lieutenant and his "grand coup." He sent Bill to watch the road — not because he expected any cars to come by, but to keep him from listening in. He and Bron sat down in the skiff and Chester really let himself go on the subject of the lieutenant. He blew his stack, so he said, and when he'd finished, he felt better than he had for weeks.

"No use crying over spilt milk," he said, "and nobody's been shot, and I don't have to worry about you anymore, or the lieutenant either. He's sure to be replaced when the brass hears about this." He slapped Bron on the back again to emphasize his relief. "Let's go now and send those poor fellows on the hill home."

Distinctly, Chester and Bron heard a car coming toward them along Haskell Street. They hurried to join Bill at the top of the bank by the side of the road. Blasts from the motor alternated with squeals from the brakes and the grinding of gears. Two murky blobs of light lurched out of the blackness, hesitated, made a jab to the right, a jab to the left, and with a roar charged head-on at the men on the bank. They jumped aside. A delivery van hurtled down the bank, across the intervening beach, and finally stalled and stuck in mud and a couple of feet of water. The men picked themselves up and stumbled after the van. Chester, with his hand on his pistol, waded out to the cab and flashed his torch through the window on the driver's side. The white and terrified faces of a boy and a girl stared out at him. Chester took his hand off his pistol and opened the cab door. The boy who had been driving rolled off the seat into Chester's arms.

"There, there," said Chester. "Don't be frightened. We're the police." The boy made no sign. He had fainted.

Meanwhile Bill had waded out, opened the door on the other side, and been nearly knocked flat by the girl who jumped out.

"Now, now, sister," said Bill, as he struggled and splashed to hold on to the girl. "Don't fight so! You're getting us all dirty and wet."

Chester carried the boy back to the beach and laid him out on a patch of marsh grass. He groaned, and again Chester spoke gently to him, "Nothing to worry about. We're just the police."

Chester's remark seemed to reassure the girl. She let Bill lead her to shore.

"Oh, Officer," she cried, "I was so frightened, but now I'm better, and I'll just run home because it's late, and my father will be waiting up for me. He's terribly old-fashioned. He always waits up, and I hate to worry Daddy." She made a dive to get away, but Bill held on.

"Just tell us your name and your boy friend's name and where you live, and we'll drive you both home. It's not safe for you to be running around in this fog."

The boy sat up and muttered something about the van.

"We'll haul it out for you before the next tide. Don't worry."

"I didn't steal it," mumbled the boy. "I just borrowed it."

"That's good," said Chester.

"From my boss," said the boy.

"He'll be grateful to get it back," said Chester.

"He needs it at eight o'clock tomorrow morning."

"We'll try to haul it out by then," said Chester, "but we've got to wait 'til we can see to bring down the tow truck."

"He'll think I stole it. I'll lose my job. I borrowed it to drive down to see her, but he'll think I stole it." The boy began to cry.

"Maybe we can help you explain to him," said Chester. "Maybe it won't be so bad as you think. Now, Miss, just tell us your name and where you live."

"Please, Officer, please!" The girl's voice throbbed with anguish. "It would kill my daddy to see me brought home in a police car. Just let me walk home — I know the way — and spare poor Daddy."

"Don't be silly," said Chester. Then he added, "Don't I know you?"

"I don't think so, Officer," said the girl. "My name's Susan Hacker, and Daddy and I are visiting down on Station Avenue. I guess we missed the turn, but I can find it now all right."

"Tell the truth, Mary Cornish," said Bron out of the darkness.

"So that's who it is! I thought I knew you," said Chester. "I'll take you right up to your grandmother."

Bill Acker let out a yell. Before either Chester or Bron knew what had happened, Mary was lost in the darkness and fog. A minute later, they heard the clatter of her shoes on the road as she raced up the hill.

"She bit me," howled Bill Acker. "I'm bleeding."

Chester knew he hadn't a chance of getting the paddy wagon out of the bushes and up the hill in time to catch Mary before she dashed past the Munsons' cottage on the way to her grandmother's. He started after her at a run, tripped on the bank, and turned his ankle. He groaned and swore and yelled at Bron and Bill to get after her and stop her, quick!

"I'll take the back path," Bron shouted back. "Maybe I can cut her off."

Swearing fiercely, Bill Acker pounded up the road. Chester limped after him. He was about halfway up the hill when he heard the shots and Mary's scream.

When Chester had finished his story I offered him a cup of coffee, but he said he didn't have time. He had to see about pulling the van out of the mud, and fixing things up for Mary's boy friend. He said he had forgotten all about the kid until he was on his way home at about four in the morning. The fog had lifted, and it was getting light. He saw the van still stuck in the mud, went to look at it more closely, and found the kid asleep in the cab. He had taken him home with him, and he expected the kid was awake by now and worrying about the van and his boss.

Jerusha's Narrative

I Am a Nurse

DURING THE FOUR WEEKS that Bron was in bed at The Haven, I had all I could take of being treated like a grownup and trying to act like one. Right away, when I came down to breakfast, very late, on the morning after the shooting, Aunt Edith told me that I must be Bron's nurse. Grandpa had insisted Bron stay with us until he was better. He wouldn't hear of the hospital. Aunt Edith said that she would cook, clean, do the laundry, help me in every way she could, do anything, in fact, except see Bron. She said then, as she had before, that she never wanted to see him again.

Dr. Davis came every day. He gave his orders to me. Freddy sat with Bron sometimes in the afternoon. Grandpa sat with him at night and slept better in a chair beside Bron than in his own bed. Chester had intended to come up often to visit Bron, but he was traveling to and from Boston, New York, and even Washington, making reports about the "grand coup" that failed. He sent Bron a picture postcard every day to make up for not coming himself. Bron was very much my responsibility.

Aunt Edith and I didn't talk together in the evenings the way we had earlier in the summer. Bron had brought us together then. Our hopes and fears, our shared bit of gossip, our speculations and confessions all centered on him. Now, when Bron came into our conversation, Aunt Edith acted as if he were the patient of a medical discussion, or someone she had read about in a newspaper once, long ago. Anyway, I was too sleepy at night for confidential chats. During the day, when I came downstairs to eat or on errands, Aunt Edith discussed every subject except Bron with me as if we were equals. She never criticized or scolded me. She praised me and wrote letters in my praise to my parents. Living up to Aunt Edith's high opinion of me was an awful strain. If I complained about anything, she tried to fix it right away. Sometimes she was cross and scolded Grandpa or Freddy or Dr. Davis or herself, but never me. She urged me to take naps or walks or sails and she cooked special delicacies to tempt my appetite. I think I would have felt more comfortable if, sometimes, she had given me one of her old no-nonsense-now schoolmarm lectures. She was so kind and gentle and grateful to me for helping her over this bad time that I had to do my best, every minute, to be worthy. I felt sorry for her too because I knew that, even more than I, she was hurt by what Bron had done.

Nursing Bron was a strain, too, but he didn't set any high standards for me to live up to. In fact, he seemed to me to be indulging in all the childishness I was having to forgo. After the first few days, he began to run a fever. Dr. Davis said he had a respiratory infection which might develop into pneumonia. He came twice a day until the fever went down and was very particular about how I carried out his orders. He said that everything depended on my keeping Bron warm and quiet, getting him to drink plenty of liquids, giving him his medicines on schedule, and checking his temperature regularly.

From the first, Bron had seemed to me to resent everything I tried to do for him. Most of the time, luckily for me, he was very weak. He lay quietly against his pillows and whispered to me to stop pestering him with soup and pills and thermometers and leave him to die in peace. In the late afternoons, though, when his fever was at its height, he got restless and almost wild. One day he knocked the thermometer right out of my hand and broke it. On another he threw back his covers, exclaiming that they were like a huge, hot flatiron pressing him down. I brought him another, lighter blanket, and he threw that off too, muttering things I couldn't understand and glaring at me. He sat straight up as if he were going to climb out of bed. I tried to push him back, and he pushed me away.

"Where is she?" he demanded. "What have you done with her?"

I guessed he meant Mrs. Munson. "She had to go away very suddenly," I said.

"Why?"

"I — I'm not sure why," I faltered. Remembering the letter that Mary hadn't delivered, and hoping to quiet Bron, I added, "She wants you to trust her and wait."

He seemed relieved. He leaned against his pillows, let me cover him again, and soon fell asleep.

Bron weak and feverish was easier to nurse than Bron convalescent. As soon as he felt better he told Dr. Davis, very rudely, to get him some crutches. He wanted to walk down to the cove and live aboard *Irene* again where he'd be safe from medicines and thermometers and other indignities. Dr. Davis explained very carefully and scientifically why Bron must stay in bed another two weeks before he could try to walk with crutches. Bron cursed him, using words I had never heard before. Dr. Davis walked out of the room. I guess he was afraid that if he stayed he would lose his temper, too.

Later Dr. Davis telephoned me to say that from now on he was only coming to see Bron once a week, but would telephone me every morning and evening. I was to report to him then and take down his instructions. In case of emergency, I was to telephone him right away. He gave me his telephone numbers at home, at the office, and at the hospital. He was a very conscientious doctor. Bron said that since Dr. Davis was determined to keep him a prisoner, the least I could do was get him a few of his own things out of *Irene*. Between us, during the afternoon, Freddy and I made at least ten trips to and from *Irene* bringing things Bron thought he wanted that weren't there, or that Bron decided, once he had them, he didn't want after all. Finally Freddy burst into tears. Bron realized how mean he had been, and he burst into tears too. So did I. We came together in a three-way embrace on the bed, only I had to dash away to answer the telephone. It was Dr. Davis wanting my evening report.

The next morning, still in a repentant mood, Bron begged me to bring him the ugly quilt we had found up in the cupola. "I know you hate it," he said, "but I've been thinking how your dear grandmother sewed it when she was a prisoner in this room, just the way I **am** now. Her imprisonment was no less real for being self-imposed. My sufferings now must be like hers then. Oh, I know, Jerry" — Bron gave me a sheepish grin — "you think the sufferings I endure are nothing compared to what I inflict on you, with my moods and tantrums, and I don't blame you. I'm a pain in the neck. I do suffer, though, and now maybe I can understand, as I couldn't before, why your grandmother sewed the quilt and kept it and wanted it when she felt she was about to die. I'm sure it is what she wanted."

Bron paused in thought. "I keep remembering the look in her eyes when she was trying to tell us to get her a quilt. It was so unlike her, and this quilt is unlike her, too, and unlike all the other quilts she sewed. You see, Jerry, there is a connection between the quilt and the way she looked, if I can only find out what it is. Come on, Jerry," he coaxed, "get it for me. I promise I'll behave and be a good patient, and if I can't find this connection I'm looking for, I'll let Edy burn the quilt when she gets back — which is what you and she have been wanting to do right along. By the way," he added, "when is she coming home?"

I realized then that Bron, in his fever, had somehow mixed up what I told him about Mrs. Munson with Aunt Edith. Or perhaps he hadn't mixed anything up. Perhaps he had been asking about Aunt Edith, and I had misunderstood him. I had often wondered that he hadn't asked where she was and why she hadn't been in to see him, and I had dreaded telling him that she never wanted to see him again. Flustered, and anxious to avoid another scene, I just muttered something about not being sure and ran off to find the quilt.

Ugly and sinister as it was, it saved me that time from having to tell Bron the truth, and for the next two days it kept Bron so absorbed he didn't ask about Aunt Edith again. When he wasn't examining the quilt, stitch by stitch, or feeling it over, or even sniffing at it, he was staring straight ahead at nothing and concentrating. At night we put the quilt in a bureau drawer so Grandpa wouldn't see it and be disturbed. Those were two of the easiest days I had with Bron. On the third day I came in with his lunch tray to find him flat on his back on the floor, staring groggily at the ceiling. I tugged at him with all my strength but I couldn't lift him. For once, maybe because he was dazed, he cooperated. Between us we got him back into bed. Since there didn't seem to be much the matter with him, and he begged me not to call in Dr. Davis, I didn't. Bron was grateful to me, and the next morning he even said he was sorry for the trouble he'd caused me and explained how he came to fall.

After he had concentrated on the quilt for two days without discerning the faintest glimmer of the connection he was looking for, he did come up with a useful idea. To make the illuminating connection between Grandma's terror and the quilt, he needed a catalyst. The catalyst might be anything — a letter, a book, a scrap of cloth or paper, or a remark by someone who had once seen or heard something. It could be anywhere in The Haven or in Sewell for that matter. Most likely it was lost or destroyed. Bron said he would have given up right then, appalled by the needle-in-the-haystack aspect of his quest, if his eye hadn't lighted on the golden Gothic lettering on the backs of the old books in my bookcase. It was the same Gothic lettering on the same old books that caught the morning sun and delighted me when I was a child. Bron guessed what I had always known: that the books had belonged to Grandma when she was a girl.

"Don't give up," he told himself, "until you've had a look

at these." And in his eagerness, forgetting how weak he was (and the doctor's orders), he climbed out of bed and fell.

I brought him the books and piled them all around him on the bed and the table beside the bed. Reading through them, looking for his catalyst, kept him busy for another two days. Finally, he told me to put them all back in the bookcase, except for one which was a textbook of Pitman shorthand. It had Grandma's name on the flyleaf and must have been the book she used at business school.

"I've about given up on the quilt," said Bron, "but this is something she knew about and I don't, and shorthand is a useful tool, and studying shorthand will keep me quiet and out of your hair until Edy gets back and can help you. By the way, when *is* she coming back? I didn't know she was planning a long visit, but of course I didn't see much of her this summer." Bron frowned and a wistful note came into his voice. "She didn't tell me her plans. There was no reason, of course, why she should."

I should have told him then, but I didn't have the nerve. Again I pretended I didn't know.

For the next four days Bron concentrated on learning shorthand. He sat up with the ugly quilt spread over the bottom of the bed — to keep him, he said, from forgetting about it. He read and memorized and scribbled down the shorthand symbols so hard and fast that he had finished the first ten lessons by the afternoon of the first day. Then he made me give him dictation for two hours. Each day he worked harder and faster. I wouldn't have believed that anyone could get so fired up for so long about anything as dull as shorthand. He didn't notice when I showed him the crutches that Dr. Davis had sent up for him to practice on. He didn't hear any-

thing I said except when I was dictating to him out of the
book. He forgot to eat his meals. He began to look as pale
and thin as he had the first days after he was shot. When he
announced that he was going to study nights, too, I telephoned
Dr. Davis. He brought up some sleeping pills which I got
Bron to eat by telling him they would help him stay awake
and study. That, after all, was what Grandpa said Dr. Davis's
sleeping pills did, so I was not really lying. Bron fell asleep
over his shorthand before I had even got Grandpa settled in
the room with him for the night.

The next day Bron was furious with me for deceiving him.
He told me to get out of his room and stay out until he called
for me. I got mad then, too. I told him he had a nerve saying
the room was his when it was mine, and he would call a long
time before I came to him. I stamped out. I got some books
and some gum out of Freddy's drawer, and I spent the morning
(it was warm and sunny again) lounging in the arborvitae
jungle. It was wonderful just to be lazy for a change.

"I hope you got a sail, Jerry," said Bron when I returned.
"You've been cooped up with me and my bad temper too long.
You deserve some fun for a change." He had piled up all his
papers and books neatly on the table beside him. He had
folded the ugly quilt up small and held it on his knees. He
had combed his hair and put on clean pajamas. He smiled
as if my coming back really made him happy. My heart
throbbed — almost as it had, so long ago it seemed now, when
a smile from Bron was like a glimpse of heaven to me.

"I didn't feel like a sail, so I just lay under the arborvitae
and chewed gum and read a little and looked out over the
river the way I used to when I watched for you to come back
in *Irene*." I stopped, feeling foolish. What was the point of

harking back to the old times or the old Bron, or the old me? All of them were gone.

"You'll have time to sail again now," said Bron, "and maybe you'll take me along sometimes. She's back, you know, and she'll help you, and I'm almost well." Again Bron smiled as if he really found me pleasing. "You've been great, Jerry, you really have. Edy'll be proud when I tell her what a magnificent job you've done of managing me, and I've got something else to tell her, too. I don't know how she'll take it.

"Call her up, quick, Jerry, please, like a good girl. I can't wait any longer. She must have got back just now while you were hidden in your jungle because you left the door open, and I heard her step downstairs."

I felt cold and a little sick. I knew I couldn't fool him any longer. "She's been here all the time," I said.

Bron looked what Grandma used to call "flabbergasted." "You told me she had gone away for a visit."

I took a deep breath. "I didn't mean to lie. I wasn't lying at first because when you asked for Aunt Edith I thought you were asking" — I hesitated, but finally got it out — "for Mrs. Munson."

"Oh, that," said Bron. "I see." After a long pause, he added, "So Edith has been in the house all the time I've been sick, but she's never once been up to see me?"

"After what you've done," I said, "she says she never wants to see you again."

Bron winced. "She's a hard woman," he said. "Other people give me the benefit of the doubt. After all, there is no evidence against me. Only Edith is too proud . . ." He broke off. After a moment he added, "I'm surprised she has let me stay here at all."

I explained how Grandpa had insisted that Bron stay at The Haven until he was well, and how Aunt Edith and I divided the work so that she helped me even though she didn't have anything to do with Bron. He said, "How cleverly she preserves the amenities without soiling her immaculate self."

I wasn't sure what Bron meant by this, but his voice and his eyes were so hard that I felt I must put in a word for Aunt Edith.

"You did deceive her, Bron. She's very unhappy about it. I know she is."

Bron glanced down at the ugly quilt folded on his lap. He looked up at me with hard eyes and a funny smile. "Don't make excuses for her. There's a vindictive streak in the females of your family. That's clear, and Edith's got it worst of all." Bron gave a harsh laugh. "It seems to have missed you, Jerry." His voice and eyes softened. "You've been very good to me. Thank you."

He sighed, looked down at the quilt again, then around my room, and finally back at me. "I'm not hungry, and I don't need anything. Chester's coming to see me later. In his last postcard he promised he'd come today. I'll do a little writing until then. You run along to your jungle, or have a sail, or anything you like. There's a good girl." He smiled his old, gentle smile at me, and then forgot me (I could tell) for his own thoughts. I was relieved to have come through that ordeal.

Gone

AUNT EDITH WAS OUT but she had left some lunch for me in

the kitchen. After I had eaten I wandered into the yard. There wasn't wind enough to rustle the leaves of the wisteria, let alone sail my boat. I crawled through the arborvitae jungle and took the back path down to the cove. In the four weeks I'd been cooped up, the wild roses had given place to early goldenrod. The marshes below were more brown now than green, clouded with patches of sea lavender. Haze blotted out the horizon and dimmed the sparkle of the water. The black *Irene* and my white catboat, the shiny newness of their paint weathered away, hung motionless and a little shabby on their moorings. The cove, so bright and glancing when I'd seen it first that summer on a breezy afternoon in June, was subdued today and, it seemed to me, tinged with sadness. I calculated that in about a week Freddy and I must go home to Chicago. Bron would have to be up and out of The Haven by then. I knew I should go back and start him practicing on his crutches, but I lingered to skip pebbles, and dream about the cove in the old, bustling days Grandma had told me about, and to think about Grandma too. I was ashamed that in the past weeks I had thought so little about her. I felt that I had been disloyal.

I wandered along the base of the hill, as I had so often with her, picking sea lavender, inspecting the wild beach-plum bushes — the plums were still green — and looking for the big old mullein plant known to Grandma and me as Mr. Mullen. It was there, shooting up above the goldenrod, just as it had been when Grandma and I first discovered and named it long ago. Every year we used to measure my height against Mr. Mullen's. Only last summer Grandma and I had measured me, and I had been childishly proud to find myself as tall as he. In memory of Grandma I measured myself now, as best I could by myself. I was at least two inches taller than Mr. Mullen. As

I sauntered back to the path and climbed the hill toward home,
I thought about how different I was now from the little girl of
a year, or even of two months ago.

I found Bron busily writing. He said Chester had helped him
practice on the crutches and had only just left. As soon as he
had finished what he was writing, Bron said, he would like to
practice some more. He did so well on the crutches that, since
Aunt Edith was still out, I suggested he try going up and down
the stairs. He managed the stairs without mishap and, when
we were safely back in the room, he said, "Do you remember at
the beginning of the summer how we started out on an ice-
cream sail to Houghton Landing and turned back because we
figured out where the quilt was hidden?"

I remembered.

"You can put the quilt away or throw it away, or whatever
you like. I'm through with it, but I would still like to sail to
Houghton Landing with you and buy an ice-cream cone. Do
you think you could help me down to the cove tomorrow and
sail us over the way we were going to?"

"Oh, yes," I said, "let's try it."

There was a wind next morning, and we got off early while
Aunt Edith was dusting Grandpa's study. I left her a note telling where we had gone and when we'd probably be back, so
she could keep out of the way and not see Bron. Bron was
pretty tired when we got to the cove. He said he was glad he
didn't have to row, and he asked me to row the skiff once
around *Irene* before we boarded the catboat. He held on to
Irene's gunwale for a few minutes while he looked into the
cockpit, then he said something I couldn't understand — in
Polish, I guess — patted *Irene*'s hull, and told me to row on.
He needed lots of help to climb aboard the catboat and get

comfortably settled. I raised the sail, cast off, and tacked down the river into the harbor. There a fresh southeast breeze smacked into us, and I got so interested in my sailing that I forgot about everything else. We made Houghton Landing in two hours, which was good time against a head wind. We tied up at the town pier, I helped Bron out of the catboat, and he hobbled on his crutches to King's, the ice-cream and candy store. We ate our cones sitting at one of the tables in the store so that Bron could rest. He asked the salesgirl if she knew how he could get a taxi; when she said, sure, she would call the number for him and the taxi would be around in a few minutes, he turned to me.

"While I'm here, Jerry," he said, "I would like to drive over to the Catholic cemetery and look at the graves of my parents. I haven't been there for a long time. I want to go alone. You won't mind waiting a little while, will you? It won't take very long."

I said I wouldn't mind.

"That's a good girl." Bron smiled at me. "While I'm gone, you pick out two pounds of chocolates for you and Freddy to eat on the train on your way home. I'll pay for them now, along with the cones."

Bron paid the salesgirl. The taxi arrived. Bron got in, waved to me, and was driven away. The salesgirl didn't have any other customers, and she let me take my time about choosing the chocolates I wanted. She even gave me free samples when I couldn't decide between Needhams and nougats. It hardly seemed any time at all before the taxi came back. The driver came into the store with three envelopes in his hand.

"I guess you're the girl, all right," he said, and handed the

envelopes to me. One had my name on it, one had Grandpa's, and one had Aunt Edith's.

"Where is he?" I asked.

"Don't worry," said the taxi driver, "I got him on the eleven fifty-three out of the junction. He was afraid he'd stayed so long at the cemetery that he'd miss the train, but the conductor's a friend of mine. He saw us coming and waited a minute, and we helped him get aboard." The driver waved to the salesgirl, said, "So long," and left.

I sat looking at the envelopes. They were bent from being carried in Bron's pocket, and the writing was smudged, I guessed from spray. I decided I'd rather open my envelope and read what was inside alone on the catboat than in the store. I forgot my candy and, as I left, the salesgirl ran after me with it.

"You okay, honey?" she asked. "You look sorta pale."

"I'm okay," I said. "And thanks. Thanks for the candy." I smiled, nodded, took the candy, and made a dash for the pier. I read my letter sitting in the catboat. It said:

Dear Jerry,

I'm not enough of a stoic to stand up "like a man," as they used to tell me when I was a boy, and say good-bye to Reverend Faunce, to Freddy, and, least of all, to you. I'd cry like a baby and embarrass you. That's why I've slipped off this way. Please forgive me, and forgive me too for all the thoughtlessness, selfishness, and ill temper I've subjected you to over the past month.

Do you remember those lovely lazy afternoons when you and Freddy and I sunned ourselves on *Irene* and exchanged confidences? How happy we were then! I said that I was going to do something distinguished to show that I was a better American than any of you. In spite of everything, I'm still proud and ambitious and honest in my way. I may have deceived you, Jerry, but I've never deceived myself. I'm off now to show what I can do on my own. If I can't come back a success, I shan't come back at all. I guess I am vindictive, too.

As for you, dear Jerry, you are better than the rest of us. Stay as you are, and try to keep a small place in your heart for me. You will always be in mine. Say good-bye to Freddy for me. Tell him that I will always love him and remember him, and that when he is a great inventor, as he surely will be someday, I hope he will sometimes remember *Irene* and me.

Your friend,
Bron

How well, indeed, I remembered those afternoons on *Irene* — the swimming, the sarsaparilla, the cookies, the delicious smell of Bron's after-shaving lotion, and, dearest memory of all, Bron himself, smiling at me, patting my shoulder, while the sun glinted on his golden hair. My memories and the flattering and loving things Bron had written to me made me cry. Out of that letter, written by the new Bron, the ill-tempered patient, the deceiver, the lover of a lady bootlegger already married to someone else, had sprung my old Bron, the one I had loved and lost, who had never existed except in my imagination anyway.

Once started I couldn't stop crying. I cried for myself, because all my feelings, and everything I had ever known or believed, were churning around inside me like an undigested meal, making me miserable. I cried for both Brons. I no longer knew which was which, but their sudden departure had left me with a terrible ache. I cried for Aunt Edith, whom I used to hate, who was my closest friend. She was getting her wish of never seeing Bron again, and yet this was almost as sad as the loss of Bron himself. I cried for Grandpa and Freddy because they were gentle and good. I cried for Sunbeam because he was a fine, old cat who had belonged to my dear Grandma who was dead. As Grandpa had said, nothing was right since she had died. Nothing was clear, or certain, or manageable anymore, and I suspected nothing ever would be again. I sat in the catboat and cried on and on until I was cried out and felt better. I didn't have a handkerchief, so I wiped my eyes and blew my nose on the edge of the sail before I raised it and cast off. I sat on the letters and the box of chocolates all the way home, so they wouldn't blow away or get wet.

Edith's Narrative

The Message of the Quilt

Wᴇɴ Jᴇʀᴜsʜᴀ ᴡᴀʟᴋᴇᴅ ɪɴᴛᴏ ᴛʜᴇ ᴋɪᴛᴄʜᴇɴ, over an hour late but safe and sound, I ran and hugged her. I never shared my mother's or Jerusha's own confidence in sailboats. If I had known in time that she was sailing with Bron — disabled as he was — all the way to Houghton Landing just for ice-cream cones, I would have tried to prevent her. It seemed to me that Bron was getting more irresponsible and selfish every day. I told Jerusha that, if he was well enough to sail to Houghton Landing, it seemed to me he was well enough to take care of himself on *Irene,* or wherever else he chose to go.

Jerusha blinked and snuffled as if she were going to cry. "He *is* well enough," she said, "and he's gone away — for good."

I made her eat something before telling me just how Bron had gone away. She showed me the letter he had written her. I was glad to see that he had written so affectionately and that he apologized for "deceiving" her, but I wondered that he made no attempt to explain himself. The "too" in the sentence "I guess that I am vindictive, too," I guessed referred to me.

"What would he have me be?" I thought. "Sympathetic?"

Angry as I was with Bron, I opened his letter to me, hoping for some explanation or word of regret that would make it easier to accept what he had done and to bear the hurt he had left with me. This is what I read:

Dear Miss Faunce:

I write concerning the quilt which was found earlier in the summer in the cupola of your house.

You will recall that shortly before she was taken to the hospital where she died, Mrs. Faunce wanted something very important brought to her. Because of motor aphasia, resulting from her stroke, she was unable to speak. She did, however, manage to write down a few words with her left hand, which was not paralyzed. The first word she wrote was definitely *quilt*. Of the two words that followed, only the first few letters were legible, *c* and *sh*. Later Mrs. Faunce tried to write again. This time only one word, *up,* and the letters *p* and *i* at the beginning of another word were legible.

The *c,* as our later discovery of the quilt proved, stood for *cupola.* I submit now that the letters *sh* and *pi* stood for the words *shorthand* and *Pitman.*

Mrs. Faunce had learned the Pitman system of writing shorthand when she was a young woman. A message in Pitman shorthand is written into the quilt which was found, after Mrs. Faunce's death, in the cupola.

In the Pitman system, consonant sounds are represented by straight or curved strokes (like the radii and arcs of a circle), either shaded or unshaded. A competent writer of

Pitman does not include vowel sounds in his script. They must be deduced by the reader from the consonant sounds and the context. In Mrs. Faunce's quilt, many of the curved and straight edges of the patches were cut and sewn together to correspond to the basic strokes (arcs and radii, shaded and unshaded) which represent consonant sounds in the Pitman system. The seams in the quilt which correspond to basic strokes are sewn in red thread — single for unshaded, double for shaded. Seams sewn in black thread represent spaces between words and are not meant to be read as part of the message.

In addition to the basic strokes representing consonant sounds, the system has some variant forms for them. These are small hooks or circles attached to the beginning or end of a basic stroke. Double and triple consonants are represented by small circles or loops. There are also some short forms for common prefixes, suffixes, and verb endings, as well as whole words, commonly used in business, which are not represented by basic consonant strokes. In the quilt, the hooks, circles, loops, etc., look like extra bits of red stitches tacked onto the beginnings and ends of seams sewn in red. The message is written from left to right and from top to bottom, but this can only be determined when the reader knows the shorthand symbols and in what order they make sense. No punctuation marks are used in the shorthand message. I have provided them in my transcription, which follows:

"Had consented to elope with Henry. Plans made, bags stowed in catboat. Would sail to Houghton Landing, drive to R.R. station, take train to Boston and New York. Henry whistled under window. Father, Mother asleep. Met him downstairs. Went to Father's office. Opened safe to take out jewelry and stocks belonging to me which

Henry needed to start own business. Henry tied handkerchief over my mouth. Bound my hands and feet. Took everything from safe and stuffed it in bag he carried. Slung me over shoulder, carried me out of house, halfway down hill. Set me on feet, untied them, showed me pistol in holster on hip, told me walk on to cove. Rowed us to catboat, sailed down river. Explained had asked me to elope because only I knew where safe hidden and combination. Would take me to Houghton Landing. Could sail home from there. Once home, could tell Father about elopement and robbery. Henry well away with money. No difference to him. Advised me keep quiet, not enrage Father, humiliate self by admitting I'd opened safe and been jilted. Horrified! Couldn't beg Henry repent because of gag. Sailed into harbor, very windy. Henry poor sailor, blown toward ledges, untied my hands, removed gag, told me sail boat. Sailed out of trouble, begged Henry repent, sail home, return money, pray God for forgiveness. Would never tell on him. Said money all he wanted. Not scared of hellfire. Laughed, shook bag of money in my face, took pistol from holster, pointed at me, told me to keep quiet and sail boat. Any funny business, he'd shoot me and throw my body in bay. Decided must kill him. Planned how. Beyond Gull Point — open ocean, stronger wind, very rough. Took chance. Sailed close to wind. Boat heeled, shipped water. Pretended was scared. Told Henry put away pistol, sit on windward gunwale prevent capsize. Henry obeyed, balanced on gunwale. Pointed boat closer into wind, came about, suddenly let sheet run, heading downwind. Boom swept Henry into water. Sailed home. Bag of money went overboard with Henry. Weak, foolish, sinful girl! Murderess! Prayed God for courage to confess what I had done. He does not hear. I cannot bring myself to tell, yet, if I do not, I do not deserve His forgiveness. This is my confession to Him. If He does not grant me courage to confess to the world, perhaps He will let this quilt be found and read, and I will be forgiven. This is my only hope. Jerusha Haskell."

If you choose to show the quilt to a competent user of Pitman shorthand, he will tell you that the above transcription is correct.

Sincerely yours,
Bronislav Zebrzycki

I handed the letter to Jerusha, sheet by sheet, as I finished each one. Perhaps I should have kept the terrible story about her grandmother from Jerusha, but I needed her sympathy and support. My shock and consternation over what I read were secondary to the pain I felt because Bron hadn't even said good-bye to me. I bent my head and tried to accept the fact that he felt tenderness and regret for everyone he was leaving, except me. For me he had only contempt. Jerusha understood my feelings. She took my hand and held it.

"It was mean of him not to say good-bye," she said.

I nodded, and we were both silent for some time.

"This about Grandma," Jerusha went on, hesitating between phrases, "doesn't really matter. Not now. Not after she didn't get the quilt when she wanted it. It doesn't change Grandma. She's just the way she always was. I believe Bron, and I believe everything happened the way he's written it, but at the same time I don't believe it. It's like a bad dream. It happened all right, but it isn't real."

"It was an aberration," I said.

"A what?" Jerusha asked.

"A mistake. She put it behind her, and it doesn't really matter. I think we shouldn't mention it to anyone."

"No, I wouldn't want to," said Jerusha.

To myself I added, "Bron was my aberration, and I must put him behind me."

I sent Jerusha off to rest, washed the dishes, and got after the ironing. The children were leaving soon, and I wanted to send them home with their clothes clean and pressed. However, my mind wandered from my work. Sometimes, in spite of all my efforts at self-control, tears came to my eyes. I ended up by burning a hole in Jerusha's good traveling dress.

Father came to supper in a somber mood. "He is gone," he said. "He wrote me a most beautiful letter of farewell, and he has left instructions with Chester to sell his boat and give the proceeds to the church as a memorial to my late, dear wife. He was always a generous lad, a bright lad. He brightened my life. I shall miss him, Edith, and so will you." Father stroked old Sunbeam who was sitting beside him as usual, waiting to be served. "He was a sunbeam in our lives," said Father with a sigh. "We could not expect him to stay with us always. He has gone to prove himself in the world. We must get on as best we can until he comes back."

A few days later Father and I saw the children off on the first leg of their journey home to Chicago.

Conclusion Ante Finem, April 15, 1945

JERUSHA AND I have finished our reminiscence. For the past six months I have been so involved in the events of the summer of 1926 that the winter of 1945 has slipped by almost before I realized it. The shock of President Roosevelt's death has brought me back to the present, but I believe that Jerusha is still lost in "the high and far-off times," as she calls them. She will have to come up for air soon. The war in Europe is all but over. Soon she must return with the little boys to her husband and her adopted country. I shall miss her and the boys more than I can say. All this winter our spare rooms have been heated and aired, and have seemed to breathe again. The Haven has hummed with life, as it did in the long ago days which Jerusha and I have been remembering. Sunshine, sea breezes, and sometimes sleet, snow, northeasters, and mud have swept into The Haven on the heels of the children, and the house and Father and I, too, are better for a little wear and tear. The staleness, stuffiness, and boredom that accumulate in a house that is kept rather than used have blown away. Laughter, shouts, and occasional screams have helped to make The Haven a real, live home again. Father hasn't minded drafts and banging doors, or even the screams. For him the children are paragons of wisdom and beauty, and Jerusha is a ministering angel. He hasn't had a cold all winter. It will be hard for him when they go.

As for me, I will resign myself to closing off part of my life, as I do the spare rooms, until the time when Jerusha and her family, and Freddy, too, will be able to come again. Now, even more than in the autumn, I feel that Jerusha's visit has been a windfall. Out of it has come this reminiscence — another windfall for me — which has turned out to be more than I'd bargained for and not what I expected.

Over the winter Jerusha and I have pieced our memories into a sort of crazy quilt which, unlike my mother's, seems to hide nothing and to reveal nothing, to be no more, indeed, than a crazy quilt. Certainly we have not solved the puzzle of Bron the way he solved the puzzle of my mother's crazy quilt. We were foolish to expect to, for the pattern hidden in the hotch-potch of the summer of 1926 had nothing to do with catalysts and codes. It was a pattern of a very different sort. It had to do with Bron and me, who, out of false pride, out of ignorance of our own and each other's true feelings, deliberately and against all our instincts and desires, wrenched ourselves apart. I blamed Bron, but I was more to blame than he. I see everything so clearly now. I wonder how I managed to blind myself for so long.

During that summer I drove Bron away. It started when I let him know that I thought him somehow my social inferior, and when I refused to show my real feeling for him. I flirted with Dick Davis, even though he bored me and I knew Bron didn't like him. When Bron began staying away from The Haven, I didn't go after him and ask him what the matter was and why he didn't come to see us anymore. I pretended not to care, and at the same time, I suspected him of misdeeds: boot-legging, being infatuated with rich summer girls at the yacht club. On evidence which convinced me at the time but seems pretty flimsy now as I think it over, I even believed he was having an affair with Mrs. Munson. I believed the worst I could about him, and I cut him off. Even when he was lying sick in this very house and I might have approached him so easily through Jerusha, I was too proud to relent. I didn't tell him that he was breaking my heart. I didn't ask him, for pity's sake, to explain himself. I drove him away as systematically as if I had wanted to. The pattern is very clear.

I can make excuses for myself: Mother's recent death and my new responsibilities had set me on edge. But excuses don't alter the fact that at the crucial time for both of us I failed Bron. I hadn't the courage to put aside my pretensions and suspicions, to overcome my reticence and my pride. I didn't go to him and ask him to love me and no one else because he meant more than all the world to me. Bron would have taken me to his heart. Of that I am sure.

When I failed Bron I lessened myself. I narrowed my possibilities and laid down my life's pattern. I have followed it ever since. My life has been useful in its humdrum way, and not unhappy, but, shared with Bron, it might have been so much more.

Jerusha's Narrative

Epilogue

Although Aunt Edith officially closed our memoir two months ago, I must add to it, whether she approves or not. The summer of 1926 didn't end when we thought it did. It is still going on now, in June 1945.

Of all the visitors who came to The Haven in the old days of my childhood, only Chester still comes. Dr. Davis left Sewell for wider and more lucrative pastures many years ago. Chester never married. Since his mother died he has lived alone, and he and Aunt Edith between them run Sewell. Chester is still chief of police and, since the start of the war and the consequent decline in business at his garage, he has been harbor master, road commissioner, chief air-raid warden, town moderator, and chairman of more committees than I can remember.

Because Chester and Aunt Edith are old friends and always have some business or other to discuss, he comes to The Haven often, either on foot or on his bicycle. He refuses to use any of his official positions to get gasoline for his car. Aunt Edith says the exercise has been good for him and that he has lost weight. To me, he hardly looks or acts a day older than he did twenty years ago. He still brings Aunt Edith raspberries and other delicacies from his garden, and for my little boys he always has a package of gum or candy or some electrical contraption that buzzes, or flashes, or rings bells. For Grandpa and me, who are quite isolated here on our hill, he brings the local news and gossip. To spare Grandpa he tempers any alarming items, just as he used to. For me I suspect he colors them up to make them more interesting.

"At last it can be told," he announced one evening in June. "First I had to wait for V-E Day, and then I had to wait for official permission to speak." He was sitting with Aunt Edith and me under the wisteria, enjoying the long twilight. Grandpa and the boys were already in bed.

For months Chester had been hinting darkly about spies and secret missions and exploits more perilous and daring than those of our rumrunners in the good old days, and right here in Sewell too, right at the foot of our hill.

"Will you tell us now?" I asked.

"Nope. Not that I couldn't. It's all declassified, as they say, but I'd rather a friend of mine told it. There's more to this tale, Jerry, than meets the eye."

"Aha," I said, to show Chester that I appreciated the suspense he was building up.

"There's history in this tale," Chester went on. "It starts back in the past, in the old days of Prohibition. I know you disapproved of rumrunning, Edy. I did myself. It was illegal, but looking back now it doesn't seem so bad as it did then, and if he hadn't then, he couldn't now." He paused and shook his head. "No use my trying to tell it, when my friend can do it so much better. He's an old friend who's visiting me, and he has a lot of education."

"You tell a story as well as anyone, Chester," Aunt Edith said. "You're just too modest. If you aren't going to tell us anything tonight, I think I'll go to bed. I'm very tired, and there is school again tomorrow."

Chester jumped to his feet. "I could bring this old friend of mine up here tomorrow afternoon, when you're back from school. He could tell the story then. How would that be?"

"You know I can never be sure when I'll get home," said Aunt Edith, "but Jerry and Father will be here to meet your friend and hear his story. If the excitement is all in the past, I'm sure Father will enjoy a tale of adventure and not be upset. I'll come along as soon as I can." She turned to the door. Chester stepped in front of her.

"I want you to be here, too, when we come." He looked at her so earnestly that she glanced at me in a puzzled way. I could only shrug and shake my head to show that I was puzzled, too.

"I don't know what's got into you, Chester," she said, "but, unless there's a catastrophe at school, I'll be home by five. Bring your friend up then. I'll be happy to meet him."

The next afternoon was so warm and fine that we were all out-of-doors at five o'clock. Grandpa was in back pottering in the victory garden. The boys were whooping and racing in and out of the arborvitae jungle. Aunt Edith was setting out red, white, and blue petunia plants in the bed around the flagpole. I was on a ladder pruning dead branches out of the wisteria.

From my height, I spotted Chester and his friend on the road, halfway up the hill. They were standing, evidently talking. Chester linked his arm in his friend's, and they walked on toward us. Chester's friend was tall, though not so tall as Chester, nor yet so broad, and as the two walked on, I had the impression that the friend was hanging back while Chester was shoving him on. I looked at him more closely. His hair was gray, but he stood straight, moved easily, and at one point nearly wrenched himself free of Chester's arm. He was too well dressed, it seemed to me, to be one of Chester's local friends, and yet something about him was familiar and associated in my mind with Sewell. Puzzled, I watched Chester ease him around the curve in the road, trundle him forward, and with a mighty effort, wheel him into our driveway.

At this point the friend threw back his head and laughed. The sun fell full on his face and I knew beyond a doubt that he was Bron. He saw me, waved, and called something. I waved too, then gripped the ladder to steady myself. Bron's head turned from me. He stood in his tracks, then ran forward toward Aunt Edith, who was running to him, dropping trowel and garden gloves as she ran. They met and embraced and clung together for so long that I had climbed down the ladder and Chester had come up beside me before they separated. They embraced again and again, and between embraces gazed into each other's eyes and murmured and laughed and sobbed.

Chester and I glanced at each other and retreated toward the house, but Bron called to us over Aunt Edith's shoulder. "Wait for me, Chester and Jerry, please wait. I came to see you and Reverend Faunce too, but first we've got so much to say — and to settle — Edy and I." He drew his arm tighter around Aunt

Edith. "We'll take a walk," he said, "around the hill. We won't be gone long, not very long. We've got to talk, but I must talk to all of you too, so wait, and don't be angry."

Chester flapped his big hand at Bron and laughed. "Don't mind us," he said. "Take your time."

"What I've been through," he said to me. "I was supposed to prepare her, but she wouldn't let me. Then, at the last minute, he would have backed out if I'd let him. But I guess it will all come out right in the end."

Grandpa took the announcement of Bron's return with serenity. He had always expected him. After all, was this not his home? However, having waited twenty years for Bron, Grandpa was not prepared to wait another hour. He and the two boys fussed and fidgeted so and demanded so many times to know when Bron and Aunt Edith were coming back, when did we *think* they were coming back, that Chester, to keep them quiet, offered to tell the tale of spies and adventure about which he'd been hinting for so long. Chester built a fire in the parlor, I made Grandpa a cup of tea to soothe him (I was waiting supper until Aunt Edith and Bron came back), and we drew our chairs around the fire. Chester took a boy on each knee, produced two Hershey bars from his pocket, and began his tale.

In the previous November, Chester had been visited secretly by a very high official in the United States intelligence service. This man — Chester had promised not to tell his name — had asked Chester's help in capturing six Nazi saboteurs who were to be landed in Sewell from a German submarine sometime in March. The mission of the saboteurs was to blow up the power systems and poison the water supplies of six large American cities. This would be a last-ditch attempt by the Nazi government to boost German morale, and to gain time for the German army to regroup and fight a little longer. Because of the brilliant work of one American secret agent, the Nazi plans were known to our authorities. At his special request, this same agent had been entrusted with capturing the saboteurs as they came ashore. He had recommended Chester as a reliable man who would help him. Chester's duties were divided into two phases. First, he was to buy and fit out a lobstering boat, from twenty-five to thirty-five feet long, with a reliable motor and a shallow draft. The high official suggested — rather pointedly, Chester thought — that the sort of boat the rumrunners had used in the old days would be particularly suitable. Once Chester had his boat readied and tied up at the town wharf (he had to manage all this as if he were planning to use the boat himself), he was to await instructions for phase two. The person who would give him his instructions would be someone he knew and trusted.

Lots of lobstering boats were for sale because their skippers were away fighting. Looking them over, Chester came upon *Irene,* renamed *Lobster Girl.* She'd been a good boat when Chester sold her for Bron some twenty years ago; and she was still a good boat, so Chester bought her. While he was putting her in shape, his thoughts often turned to Bron. He had been a clever, warm-hearted chap, and a good friend. Why had he never come back to Sewell? Suddenly, like an explosion in his head, it came to Chester that the American secret agent who was going to contact him must be Bron. Bron knew all those foreign languages, and he was a bit of a daredevil too. He would eat up cloak-and-dagger work, especially if he could do it in a boat, at night. Chester laughed.

"I was right," he said. "Bron had hand-picked Sewell Harbor for those Nazis. He'd convinced them it was the safest place on the whole east coast for them to land, and they'd sent him ahead to make the final arrangements." Chester laughed again. "Before Bron even turned up in my bedroom in the middle of the night (he hoped he'd surprise me and scare me a little, but he didn't) I'd pretty well figured out his plan. He was going to ferry in those saboteurs from the submarine just the way he used to ferry in the booze from the feeder ships, and then truck them up to where they'd be arrested. Bron was so tickled to have *Irene* again, I thought he'd rouse the neighbors, laughing and shouting, hugging me, and cavorting around my room, bumping into the furniture. He hadn't changed a bit." Chester threw back his head and roared with delight. Suddenly he clamped his hand over his mouth. He glanced at Grandpa, then at me, then scowled at the floor. He shifted his hand from his mouth to rub the back of his neck.

"I didn't mean to bring up that old rumrunning business. I guess I was carried away. There never was any evidence against him. You couldn't prove a thing. It was just that I knew, and he knew I knew." Chester shot a quick look at Grandpa and lowered his eyes again. "I hope none of you will feel different about Bron, now that you know. It was a long time ago, and if he hadn't had all that experience bringing in booze, he couldn't have brought in those saboteurs and got them arrested the way he did."

Chester turned to Grandpa again and for a moment managed to look him in the eye. Grandpa stared right back at Chester as if he were affronted.

"I've disturbed Reverend Faunce," said Chester to me in a loud and anguished whisper. "I could bite out my tongue."

"If *you* aren't disturbed," said Grandpa, "I can't understand why you think I should be. Establishing guilt and punishing it has never been my line. I deal in forgiveness."

Relief lighted Chester's large face. "Of course, sir. I should never have doubted you."

"What does disturb me," Grandpa went on, "is the time Edith and Bron are taking for their walk. It is inconsiderate of them. Little Jerusha, let me have another cup of tea. Chester, don't sit there dreaming. Get on with your story. It helps to pass the time."

Bron had stored his radio equipment and car in the garage of Cousin Harriet's cottage. He had gone out in *Irene,* taken the saboteurs off the submarine, and brought them into our cove. He had driven them to South Station in Boston. As each saboteur had boarded the train for his assigned city, he had been arrested. Chester couldn't praise Bron enough. He had done it all so quietly and efficiently. I asked him what his own part in phase two had been, and Chester admitted that there had been a hitch. At the last minute the Nazis had sent another agent along with Bron, to help him, they said. Actually he was there to kill Bron as soon as Bron had landed the saboteurs (which only he could do) and to dispatch them by new routes (about which Bron hadn't been told) to their respective cities. Bron had sensed for some time that the Nazis didn't trust him anymore. He had wanted Chester on hand to finish up the job, in case he (Bron) couldn't. Fortunately, Chester was able to finish off the second agent as he was about to stick a knife in Bron's back. The fact that all this had happened just outside of Cousin Harriet's garage — Bron was getting the car, while the saboteurs waited at the foot of the hill — and that we hadn't heard a sound gave Chester great pleasure.

She was just his boss. He was more capable than the other fellows who worked for her, and she consulted with him and relied on him. That was all. He says the Munsons weren't so bad either. They were just trying to get a start in life, and so was he. They were ambitious and reckless, but they weren't bad." Aunt Edith caught her breath. "I was the one who was bad. How could I believe what I did about him? How could I be so stupid and so cruel?" She sobbed.

I jumped up and hugged her. "It doesn't matter now," I said. "He came back. That's all that matters."

Aunt Edith kissed me, then drew away and blew her nose. "We will get married as soon as Bron can arrange for Freddy to get leave and come home for the wedding. I wish William could come too, Jerusha, but Bron hasn't so much influence with the British authorities as with our own."

I too wished that William could come, but I knew that I would rejoin him soon, and I was overjoyed at the prospect of seeing Freddy before I left.

"Bron must have a lot of influence with the navy" — I laughed — "to be able to get special leave for a plain lieutenant like Freddy."

"He has," replied Aunt Edith, and her voice rang with love and pride. "He has been promoted to a very high position. He has received medals and citations. He has been offered an important peacetime job, but he is going to resign from all that as soon as he can. He is not sure yet what he wants to do, only that we will live here at The Haven, very simply. Oh Jerusha, I shall be so proud to be Mrs. Bronislav Zebrzycki, and you must bring William and the boys here every summer, and Freddy will come too. Bron and I will pay all the traveling expenses. We insist on it."   524867

Chester laughed. "Well, sir, Bron has come back a hero, and I guess it's taking him a little time to tell Edy all about it, but he'll be along soon. I'm sure of that."

Grandpa was in no mood to be cajoled. "He would have been wiser never to have left us. Let us hope," he went on, "that from now on the nations will live in peace, and there will be no more need for such dangerous feats of heroism. We are lucky you didn't blow us all into kingdom come with those terrible explosives. Jerusha, I am losing patience. How much longer are Bron and Edith going to keep us waiting?"

Fortunately the fugitives returned a few minutes later, and, as in the old days, Bron brought with him a radiance that warmed and brightened us all. Aunt Edith was looking years younger than before her walk with Bron, and twice as beautiful. As Bron embraced Grandpa and spoke to him of his love, his gratitude for the past, and his happiness at being home again, Grandpa's spirits soared up out of petulance to the heights of beatitude. The little boys, each holding tight to one of Chester's massive thighs, eyed Bron as if he were Sir Launcelot or Robin Hood. As for me, Bron had only to smile at me and speak my name, and I was ready to fall in love with him all over again.

When Grandpa and the boys had been got to bed and Bron and Chester had left, Aunt Edith and I drew our chairs close to the embers of the fire.

"Tomorrow," said Aunt Edith, "he is going to ask Father for my hand in marriage. He insists on doing it formally." She laughed. "He thinks Father will like it that way, and he wants to be formal, too, because it is so important to him. Our engagement and marriage are not matters to be treated casually." Aunt Edith took my hand and went on earnestly. "We were all wrong about Bron, Jerusha. He never cared for Mrs. Munson.